Books by Paul Brodeur

Downstream

Paul Brodeur

Downstream

New York   Atheneum   1972

The following stories have been previously published: "The
Siphon" and "The Toll" in *The Michigan Quarterly Review;*
"Hydrography," "The Sick Fox," "The Snow in Petrograd," "The
Spoiler," and "A War Story" in *The New Yorker;* "The Turtle" in
Saturday Evening Post; "Blue Lawns" and "The Secret" in
Seventeen; and "Behind the Moon" in *Show.*

To Alan

Contents

Downstream

The Spoiler   Stephen Drew saw the
shaggy-haired skiers when he was riding up the chair
lift for his first run of the day. They came hurtling toward him over the lip of a steep face—three of them,
strung out across the trail that plunged down the mountain beside the liftline. Hatless, wearing tattered Levis
and baggy sweaters, and not deigning to make the
slightest speed checks, they came straight on, skiing
powerfully and gracelessly, bounding high into the air
from the tops of moguls and landing heavily and often
wavering off balance until, exploding off other moguls,
they seemed miraculously to regain their equilibrium in
flight. Stephen turned his attention to one skier who was
racing perilously close to the steel towers that supported
the chair-lift cable, and saw the wind-burned face of a
young man in his early twenties—a blunt, open-mouthed
face that was surrounded by a thick mane of red hair,
which, covering his ears and most of his forehead, was

3

kept out of his eyes only because it was streaming backward in the wake of his tremendous speed. The redheaded skier was past him in an instant, yet Stephen had the sensation that he had not passed beneath him but over him, like an avalanche or a jet plane. Turning in the chair, he watched the youth and his companions disappear over the lip of another face, emerge again as specks far down the mountain, and finally pass from view behind a screen of fir trees.

Stephen saw the shaggy-haired skiers again half an hour later, when he was halfway down the mountain. He had stopped to rest and was looking back to watch an instructor—a model of skiing grace—lead his class of students over a torturous series of moguls when he heard a joyous shout from far above him and, glancing up the mountain, saw the red-headed skier silhouetted, arms outflung and skis apart, against the blue January sky as he came over the lip of another face. This time, however, the youth caught an edge when he landed and, teetering out of control, plunged into the midst of the skiing class, narrowly missing a girl in yellow stretch pants before he finally righted himself and came to a ragged stop a few yards below Stephen. Now, ignoring his two companions, who, whooping at his plight, swept past and disappeared, the red-headed skier leaned forward, thrust his weight against his poles, which bent in protest, and, shaking his head as if to clear it, spat into the snow between the tips of his skis. An instant later Stephen's view of him was interrupted as the ski instructor passed between them with a straight downhill plunge and two quick finishing waggles. Placing himself directly in front of the red-

headed youth, the instructor also leaned forward on his
poles and, in a shrill German accent, began to scream
slowly spaced words that seemed to ricochet off the hard-
packed snow.

"If . . . I . . . effer . . . shall . . . see . . . such
. . . foolishness . . . again . . . you . . . shall . . .
be . . . taken . . . from . . . this . . . mount-a-a-
ahn!" he shouted in a rising crescendo of outrage. "Haff
. . . you . . . a-ahnderstood . . . me?"

For a moment the two figures remained motionless,
bent toward one another like a pair of stags locked in
combat; then the shaggy-haired skier lifted his head and
looked the ski instructor in the face. For a long time he
simply stared at the instructor without the slightest expression, but just before he pushed off down the mountain he gave a faint grin that Stephen interpreted as a
smirk of contempt.

With a surge of energy that seemed to be the residue
of anger, the ski instructor began sidestepping briskly
up the mountain to rejoin his class. When he drew
abreast of Stephen, however, he paused for breath and,
in a voice still full of rage, shouted, "They care not for
anything, this kind of people! They haff no idea what
means responsibility! If he has fallen, that one, he can
only haff badly hurt this girl in my class!"

Stephen nodded in agreement, but made no reply.
There was something in the instructor's shrilly enun-
ciated Teutonic anger that seemed improbable and out
of place on this tree-covered mountain in Vermont. Besides, Stephen had been watching the shaggy-haired
skier, who was plummeting down the mountainside with

the same reckless abandon as before, and remembering that he himself had skied with a certain abandon at the age of twenty, had been thinking with regret that the sensation of such speed was something he would never come close to experiencing again. He had, in fact, been in the process of acknowledging to himself that there were certain things he was past doing, because of fear. Not that he really wanted to ski beyond the brink of control, but to admit that he was past it and afraid to try was something else again, for, at thirty-five, Stephen considered himself a young man whose courage was still intact. Now, resuming his train of thought as the instructor resumed his climb, he realized that he envied the shaggy-haired youth who, envying no one and emulating nothing —not even the grace of ski instructors—skied only against himself, and in so doing conquered fear. Was it just a question of age? Stephen wondered. But once again the voice of the instructor intruded upon his reverie. It was a calm voice now, completely under control, and fading away as he called soothingly back to the students who trailed him down the mountain.

"So remember, always in our linked turns we lock the knees together, and we dip up . . . and then down . . . and so-o-o-o . . ."

Stephen did not see the shaggy-haired skiers on the slopes again. At three o'clock he took a final run down the mountain and found his wife, Marilyn, waiting for him outside the base lodge. She was sitting in the afternoon sun, looking very pretty in the new blue-and-white ski outfit he had bought her for the trip, and Stephen

6

paused to admire her. Then, as he bent over to release his safety bindings, he realized that she had not brought the baby with her. "How's little Petey?" he asked.

"I left him with the sitter," Marilyn said proudly, as if she were announcing an achievement. "He's fine."

Stephen kicked his boots free of the bindings. Afterward he strapped his skis together, placed them on his shoulder, and followed Marilyn through a parking lot to the place where she had left their car.

"Can we ski together tomorrow?" she asked, smiling.

"Of course!" he replied with a laugh. "Isn't that why we came up here—to ski?"

Marilyn nodded, but the smile had left her face. "The girl seems very good," she said somberly. "Her name is Janice Pike. She's got funny bleached hair, but she's intelligent and competent, and Petey took to her right away. I spent the whole morning and most of the afternoon with them, and I've given her careful instructions about everything. I really don't think we have to worry."

"Then we won't worry," Stephen replied lightly. "Does the girl know we'll want her for the next few days?"

"Yes, and she's delighted about that. Evidently she needs the money."

They had reached the car, and after fastening his skis to the roof rack Stephen got inside, opened the door on Marilyn's side, and started up the engine. As they drove through the valley that led south, toward Worthington, Marilyn continued to tell him about the sitter.

"I've given Janice the telephone number at the base lodge so we could be paged if we were needed," she went on. "She, of course, knows all the doctors in the vicin-

7

ity. Oh, and she's familiar with the house we're staying in, which makes me especially happy because of the stove and everything. It turns out the caretaker often hires her to clean up the place after weekends."

"I'd say we were lucky," Stephen said, glancing carefully at his wife. She has become more and more like me, he thought. She tries to think of all the awful possibilities.

"One thing worries me, though," Marilyn was saying.

"What's that?"

"Where the house is," she replied. "I mean it's so isolated. Not that I think anything would happen, but what if it did?"

Stephen reached across the seat and touched her arm. "Don't give in to that, baby," he said gently. But as they drove on through the valley, he realized that his words of admonition were a form of self-address. They had lost their first child—a boy of two—in an absurd accident, a year before. Little Peter had been born five months later, at the end of June, and except on rare occasions, when he had been safely tucked into his crib for the night and their neighbor, Mrs. Murphy, could come over to sit for them, they had never left him with anyone. Now, having been lent the use of a small chalet by friends in Boston, they had come skiing with the idea of spelling one another at the task of caring for the baby. (He would ski in the mornings and she in the afternoons—not an ideal solution, perhaps, but all they hoped for.) When they arrived in Worthington, the night before, they telephoned the caretaker, who came to open up the house. The caretaker was friendly and garrulous—a country handyman whose dealings with the winter sporting crowd had coated his native astuteness with a certain veneer of assurance.

"Your wife ski, too?" he asked, glancing at the baby.

"Yes," Stephen answered.

"Then you're goin' to need a sitter, ain't you?"

"Yes," Stephen replied, though he and Marilyn had scarcely bothered to discuss the possibility. "It would be nice if we could ski together," he added, glancing at her.

"I know just the girl," the caretaker said. "She's nineteen and real experienced. Lives in town. Why'nt I have her call you in the morning?"

"Fine," said Stephen. "I'd appreciate that."

After the caretaker left, he turned to Marilyn. "There's no harm in trying her out, is there?" he said.

Now, turning off the highway at a point midway between the mountain and the town, Stephen drove over a dirt road that wound up the side of the valley through thick stands of spruce and pine trees. The road was a washboard affair, bordered by high snowbanks that had been thrown up by plows, and the heavy growth had plunged it into premature shadow. There were half a dozen forks and turnoffs on the way to the house, and, realizing for the first time that none of them was marked, Stephen suddenly found himself wondering how the girl could possibly give directions to summon help. He imagined her trying to remember all the twists and turns as precious minutes slipped away. "Don't give in to that," he had told Marilyn, sitting beside him. But he had merely been talking to himself.

The chalet, a prefabricated structure with two sides consisting of panel picture windows, was hidden from the road by a wooded knoll and was reached by a narrow, rutted driveway that first passed before a similar dwelling, fifty yards away, which was unoccupied. The driveway ended in a cul-de-sac at the second house, where Stephen turned the car around and parked it. When he and Marilyn came through the door, they found the sitter watching television and Petey playing happily on the tile floor at her feet.

Ten minutes later Stephen set out to drive Janice Pike home. As they descended over the washboard road toward the valley, the girl lit a cigarette, stubbed it out, and immediately lit another. To make conversation, Stephen asked her if she had always lived in Worthington.

Janice Pike shook her head, which tossed the bleached, teased mop of hair that crowned it, and blew out a cloud of smoke. "For a year after high school I worked over to Brattleboro," she replied. "Waitressing."

"How did you like Brattleboro?"

"I like it a lot. I have a boy friend there."

"What made you come back?"

"My family," she replied. "They want me to settle down, you know?"

"What about your boy friend?"

"Oh, he drives over to see me weekends. He's a plumber's apprentice and he got himself a car this year."

They had reached the valley highway and were driving past a series of ski lodges, restaurants, and roadhouses. "I suppose there's a lot doing here on weekends," Stephen said.

"Yeah, but we just seem to drive around," replied the girl morosely, and looked out the window. "Saturday night we were driving around and I never saw so many cars parked out in front of these places," she went on. "I guess people must really be having a swell time in them. I mean little bitsy joints with just a guitar player or something and about twenty cars out front!"

Stephen glanced sidewise at Janice Pike, and decided that her hair was teased into its absurd pile as an antidote to boredom. Now he imagined her having worked over it for hours, only to drive around and look wistfully through the windshield of the apprentice plumber's car at lights in the windows of ski lodges. "You should get your boy friend to take you dancing in some of these places," he said.

"Yeah, but they're supposed to be kind of wild," she replied, with more yearning, however, than disapproval. "I mean a lot of the fellows who come skiing here are real maniacs, you know?"

"No kidding," Stephen said.

"Look, I wasn't going to say anything because your wife seems awful worried about leaving the baby and everything, but a whole carload of guys drove up to the house this afternoon. They sat out front awhile, honking and waving at me. Then they went over to the other house and left some skis and stuff inside and drove away. I'm pretty sure the caretaker doesn't know they're there, and I was a little worried 'cause they looked kind of wild, you know, but maybe they were just out for fun."

"Sure," Stephen said. "Probably a lark of some kind."

"Yeah, well, I kept the door locked anyway."

"That's a good idea," Stephen replied.

They had arrived in Worthington, a village built at

the conjunction of two roads that crossed through the mountains, and packed with shabby frame houses. Following the girl's directions, Stephen drove to the lower end of town, where, next to a small stream and the gutted remnants of a factory that had once been used to manufacture wooden boxes, there stood a particularly ramshackle dwelling with a sagging roof, peeling shingles, and a veranda that was evolving into debris. For a moment Stephen studied the house in silence; then, embarrassed, he took out his wallet and turned to the girl. "How much do we owe you, Janice?" he asked.

"Your wife picked me up at ten o'clock so that would make about six hours I worked," she replied.

"And what do you charge by the hour?" Stephen asked.

"Fifty cents?"

Stephen looked again at the decrepit house, and winced. "Tell you what, Janice, let's call it eight hours," he said, handing her four one-dollar bills. "I'll come by for you tomorrow morning at nine."

"Oh, lovely!" she cried. "Thank you!" Now, jumping out of the car, she climbed the porch steps and, skirting a large hole where several rotten planks had fallen through, waved at Stephen and went into the house.

"Thank *you!*" Stephen called after her. A child of Appalachia, he thought as he turned the car around and headed back through town. He drove more quickly on the return trip, anxious to take a bath, have a drink, and play with Petey before his bedtime. He was happy with anticipation. For the first time in a year he sensed that he and Marilyn were on the brink of resuming life. He told

himself that it was a good thing they had decided to
come skiing, and that they had been able to bring themselves to leave little Petey with the girl. They must not
give in to the temptation to overprotect him. Yes, above
all, they must not allow his life and theirs to be forever
colored by tragedy. Entangled in these thoughts, Stephen
was surprised when, fifteen minutes later, he came upon
a black Volkswagen sitting in the driveway that led up to
the house. The Volkswagen was badly battered at the
fenders and wore a bent Florida license plate, and it had
been parked carelessly, in such a way that it half blocked
the drive. Putting his car into second gear, Stephen drove
slowly around it; then, glancing toward the porch of the
other house, he saw that there were three young men
sitting on it in deck chairs. The young men were drinking beer from cans, and, looking closer, Stephen saw
that one of them was, unmistakably, the shaggy, red-
headed youth he had seen on the mountain. None of the
young men bothered to look at the passing car, but as
Stephen drove by, the redhead gave a flip of his wrist
that sent his beer can over the porch railing and into a
snowbank.

When he drew up before the house of his friends,
Stephen parked the car, got out, and stood beside it for
several minutes as he tried to decide what the three
shaggy-haired skiers were doing in the other chalet. Perhaps the caretaker is allowing them to stay there in return for some chores, he thought. Or perhaps the caretaker is making money on the side with an illicit rental.
But what if, as Janice Pike seemed to imply, the young
men had simply broken into the place? Stephen thought

13

of them catching sight of Janice's bleached hair through the picture window, and for a moment he toyed with the idea of telephoning the caretaker. Then he decided against it. Their honking at Janice was like their skiing, the parking of their car in the middle of the driveway, and the red-headed youth's disposal of his beer can. It was thoughtless, nothing more—just thoughtlessness. You're getting old, Stephen told himself. What's the point of spoiling other people's fun? But when he went into the house, he did not mention the presence of the shaggy-haired skiers to Marilyn.

In the morning the sun was shining brilliantly in a cloudless sky. When Stephen left the house to pick up Janice Pike, the black Volkswagen was still parked before the other chalet. It was there when he returned with the girl, half an hour later, so he asked her if it was the same car that had honked at her the day before.

She took a deep drag on her cigarette, and nodded. "Yeah, that's the one," she replied. "I know from the dented fenders. They must be wild drivers, huh?"

Stephen looked quickly at Janice Pike. Had he detected a slight note of admiration in her voice, or was it his imagination? Everything was "wild" to this country girl, or was it simply that, out of sheer boredom, she hoped her life might become so? "Look, Janice," he said. "I don't want to mention anything about this to my wife, but on the other hand I don't want to spend my day worrying, either. So I'll speak frankly to you—O.K.?"

"Sure, but you don't have to worry, Mr. Drew. I'll keep the door locked—you can count on that."

"Fine," Stephen said, and glanced at her hair. "But maybe you'd better stay away from the window as much as possible. I mean, just don't be sitting too conspicuously next to it."

"Oh, sure," the girl replied. "O.K."

"And I'll phone you every couple of hours from the base lodge," Stephen said. "Just to make certain things are all right."

When they went into the house, Marilyn went over a list of things she had made out for Janice to do. "Petey's lunch is on the stove," she said. "You'll just have to heat it up. If he balks at eating the beef mush, dip each spoonful into his banana-dessert mush. It sometimes works. He woke up at seven this morning, which means he'll be ready for his nap any time now. After lunch, of course, he'll take another nap. If it's still sunny when he wakes up from that one, bundle him into his snowsuit and take him outside for some air."

"No," Stephen said quickly. "Don't have him go out today."

"But if it's nice and sunny—"

Stephen shook his head, picked up an armload of jackets, poles, and ski boots, and started out the door. "A day or two won't matter," he said over his shoulder. "And I'll feel better if he stays inside."

When Stephen reached the car, he put the jackets, poles, and boots into the back and climbed in behind the wheel. He was about to start the engine when he heard the sharp crack of a rifle. The report sounded close by, but in the cold, dazzling brilliance of the morning light he could not be sure how close. Leaving the car door

15

open, he listened intently, heard several more shots, and recognized the explicitly neat sound of a .22-caliber rifle. The shots seemed to be coming from the far side of the next house, but he could detect no movement there. When Marilyn climbed into the car, he started up the engine and drove slowly down the driveway.

"Really, Stephen, you shouldn't interfere that way," Marilyn said. "Why on earth shouldn't the girl take Petey out for some air?"

"There's a reason," Stephen said absently, but they were drawing abreast of the other house, and he was not paying Marilyn any real attention, for at that moment the three young men, led by the shaggy red-headed youth, came around a corner from the back. The redhead was carrying a rifle, which, when he saw the car, he seemed to thrust out of sight between his body and the wall of the house. They must be there illegally, Stephen thought. He wondered if Marilyn had seen the weapon, but a moment later he realized that she had not.

"Goodness!" she exclaimed. "Who are *they*—beat-niks?"

Stephen nodded his head, and turned to study the young men as he drove past. Unshaven and bleary-eyed, they seemed to have recently risen after a night of heavy drinking, and now they gave the car bold looks of appraisal that, because of their brazenness, also seemed to be defensive. Looking back, Stephen saw them duck quickly into the house. He was more certain than ever now that they had broken into it, but as he continued down the drive it was the rifle that stayed in his mind. He knew that it was against the law in almost every state

16

to shoot a rifle so close to inhabited places. He wondered
if he should not call the police.

"What's the matter?" Marilyn asked.

"Nothing," he told her.

His mind, however, was in ferment. The harsh vibra-
tions of the washboard road that descended into the valley triggered his brain into conjuring up visions of catastrophe. Helplessly, he imagined the young men firing at
a beer can, the bullet ricocheting off a rock, piercing the
picture window behind which little Petey sat playing, or,
perhaps, striking the girl and causing one of her interminable cigarettes to fall, smoldering, upon a scatter rug.
. . . "They haff no idea what means responsibility," the
outraged ski instructor had said. The sentence repeated
itself within him endlessly.

"You're awfully silent," Marilyn remarked when they
reached the highway.

"It's nothing," he told her again and, stepping hard
on the accelerator, drove quickly toward the mountain,
already planning to telephone Janice Pike the moment
they arrived. The miles seemed to pass slowly, however,
and soon they found themselves behind a line of cars
bearing other skiers to the slopes. When finally they
reached the parking lot at the base lodge, he jumped
from the car, unstrapped Marilyn's skis, and handed
them to her. Then, as he reached inside the car for her
boots and poles, he deliberately pushed his own boots
out of sight beneath the seat.

"Damn!" he said, straightening up. "I've left my boots
behind."

Marilyn made a grimace of sympathy and pain.

"Why don't you take a few runs on the beginner's slope?" he asked her. "It'll get you in the swing of things. I won't be more than half an hour—forty minutes at the most."

He scarcely waited to hear her assent, but, jumping into the car, started the engine, threw it into first gear, and tore away. There was no traffic on the road leading from the mountain, but the sun, rising higher in the sky, shed a brilliant light that, rebounding from the snow and glinting off the hood of the car, found its way into his eyes. The light—a sharp, metallic intrusion—cut into him, exposing his fear as a surgeon's scalpel lays open tissue to disclose a nerve, and now, as the valley broadened, so did the range of awful possibilities that haunted his mind.

When he swerved into the driveway, twenty minutes later, he jammed the car into second gear, topped the knoll with a roar, and swept past the first chalet and the Volkswagen, which was still parked, half blocking the road, before it. He was squinting through the windshield, hoping to get a glimpse of Janice Pike's massive blond coiffure in the picture window, when dead ahead, walking toward him down the middle of the drive, he saw the shaggy red-headed youth. Stephen slammed on the brakes and brought the car to an abrupt halt; then, taking a deep breath, he was amazed to find himself filling with a curious kind of relief—the kind of relief that comes when the worst is apparent and no longer in the realm of fantasy—for the shaggy-haired youth, who was standing just ahead of the front bumper and looking at him without expression, was holding a rifle over his shoulder with one hand and the hind legs of a blood-spattered snowshoe hare with the other. Stephen's gaze traveled along the barrel of the rifle that, draped carelessly over the young man's shoulder, was pointing in the direction of the picture window, where he could see Janice Pike, holding little Peter. He got out of the car, walked toward the red-headed youth, and stopped directly in front of him.

"Is the rifle loaded?" he asked. He was looking into the young man's eyes, which were deep blue, and the sound of his voice came back to him as an alien presence —a cold breath that was still as the icicles hanging perilously from the roof of the house.

The shaggy-haired youth made no reply, but gave the snowshoe hare a shake so that—as if gore were in itself sufficient answer—its bloody carcass was swung ever so slightly in Stephen's direction.

"Look where the rifle's pointing," Stephen said. Every instinct in him wanted to make a lunge for it, but fear of causing the weapon to discharge deterred him, and this terrible fear, plus the studied unconcern of the young man's face, unnerved him. He felt his control unraveling like a ball of twine. "Damn you," he said in a hoarse whisper. *"Look where it's pointing!"*

The shaggy-haired youth gave a quick sidewise glance toward the picture window; then he looked at Stephen again and shrugged. "Relax," he said. "The safety's on."

Cursing him, Stephen told him to take the rifle off his shoulder.

For a moment the shaggy-haired youth looked at Stephen with the same detachment with which he had

19

stared into the face of the angry ski instructor; then, with taunting slowness, he swung the rifle from his shoulder in a lazy arc and rested the tip of the barrel against the top of his shoe. "Man, you've gone and lost your cool," he told Stephen, and calmly pulled the trigger. Afterward he gave an insolent grin and, to further affirm the fact that the safety was on, allowed the weight of the rifle to be suspended from his forefinger, which was still curled around the trigger.

Stephen looked at the unafraid, contemptuous face before him and, a second later, struck it. The blow—a roundhouse swing—landed just in front of the ear on the sideburn and knocked the shaggy-haired youth into a sitting position in the middle of the driveway. The rifle fell to the ground, and, stooping quickly, Stephen picked it up and pushed the safety button off.

The shaggy-haired youth had not uttered a sound, but when he saw Stephen pick up the rifle and push the safety button off, his mouth fell open, and the look of fear that Stephen hoped to see—desperately *wanted* to see—came over his face and filled his eyes. Sitting there, rubbing the side of his head with one hand and still clutching the bloody hare with the other, he suddenly looked like a small boy about to cry.

"Listen, man," he said in a voice that croaked. "Like we're low on funds, you know, and the rabbit's just for eating."

"Shut up!" Stephen replied. He wanted silence simply because he was trying to figure out what he should do next.

"So maybe it's out of season," the young man went

20

on. "What d'you care? You're not a game warden."

"Shut up!" Stephen said again, but as he looked down at the youth he felt some of the anger and hatred draining out of him.

"Look, the house wasn't even locked! It was just sitting there, like waiting for us, and the rifle was standing in the corner behind the door."

"The rabbit and the house have nothing to do with it," Stephen told him. "It's my *child*, you fool! You were pointing the rifle at my *child!*"

"But nothing *happened!*" said the shaggy-haired youth, shaking his head in puzzlement and protest. "I mean, like, if nothing's happened—"

"Something's going to happen now," Stephen told him quietly. "Here's what's going to happen. You and your friends are going to pack up and be out of here in five minutes. You are only going to have five minutes—d'you understand?—and if you are not, the lot of you, out of here for good in five minutes, I am going to make damn sure you'll be here when the state police arrive. Now get on your feet and get moving."

The shaggy-haired youth did as he was told and, still clutching the snowshoe hare, stumbled off down the driveway to the other house. A moment later Stephen saw a curtain being parted in the kitchen window and a pair of disembodied faces looking out at him. Suddenly he felt immensely weary. Glancing at his watch, he leaned against the fender of his car and waited.

Five minutes later the young men had finished packing the Volkswagen. Stephen watched them in silence as, casting nervous glances in his direction like hired men anxious to please, they threw the last of their belongings into the back of the car. He was struck by the idea that they, who had skied without fear, were now dancing to the macabre tune of his own fear, but he derived no satisfaction from it. Presently the red-headed youth came out of the house, closed the door behind him, and, picking up the hare from the porch, walked around the front of the car to the driver's side. At this point he hesitated, as if debating with himself; then he tossed the hare into some bushes and looked toward Stephen. For several moments he stood there, gazing at Stephen with profound reproach, as if what had happened between them was caused by a gulf of misunderstanding that was far too deep to ever be bridged. Then, with a sad shake of his head, he got in behind the wheel, started the engine, and drove away.

Leaning against his car, Stephen listened as the Volkswagen growled toward the valley in second gear. He continued listening until the sound of its engine faded into silence; then he turned and walked toward the house where Janice Pike, still holding the baby at the picture window, was looking out at him with horror and awe. He was thinking that he would not return the rifle to the other house until he and Marilyn and little Peter left for good. He was trembling slightly as he reached the door, but he did not know whether it was with the aftermath of rage or with a mixture of relief and regret. He told himself, however, that even now the shaggy-haired skiers were probably heading for some other mountain, where, bounding high into the air with arms outflung and whoops of joy, they would continue to escape from care.

The Turtle   The two brothers were fascinated by the pond, for it was a place where nature staged spectacles that satisfied the most savage instincts of small boys. Swallows skimmed the pond, dappling the water like skipping stones as they picked tiny insects off the surface; kingbirds chased and caught giant butterflies that undertook desperate evasive maneuvers to escape; and a belted kingfisher plunged hour after hour from the dead limb of an oak tree to spear minnows that pickerel chased inshore. Black snakes glided through the weeds, seeking frogs and baby ducks; black bass jumped for crickets and grasshoppers that tumbled off the banks; and turtles big and small sunned themselves on logs at the water's edge, and watched everything through tiny, wicked eyes.

Hiram's Pond, it was called—probably after some early settler, their father had told them, though Peter, who was eleven, and David, who was nine, preferred to think it was after the old man who tended the pumping station there that supplied water for the town. It was a small pond, half a mile long and only a couple of hundred yards across at its widest point, and it lay at the bottom of a steep hill less than a five-minute bike ride from their family's summer cottage. There were shallow parts and very deep parts in Hiram's Pond. The shallow parts were coated with lily pads that grew in sargasso-like profusion, and the deep parts lay at the foot of steep embankments that surrounded two sides of the pond. At its northern end the pond was fed by a sluggish stream that passed through a swamp studded with water-killed trees whose foreboding trunks looked like dead sentinels. Peter and David were afraid to explore the swamp because the old man who tended the pumping station said it was full of treacherous quicksand that could swallow a man in no time. They preferred the open stretches of the pond, which lay comfortably within their capacity for awe. Hour after hour they poled the old man's skiff through fields of lily pads and across deep, calm coves, fishing for bass with cane poles and bobbers, and using frogs for bait.

Peter and David caught the frogs in a pool near the pumping station, where bullfrogs, leopard frogs, and pickerel frogs bred in great numbers. The bass in Hiram's Pond were large and fought hard; some of them weighed nearly five pounds, and even the smallest ones came after the frogs with frightening voracity. Occasionally the frogs attracted turtles, which ruined the bass fishing, and when this happened the boys went to the pumping station to fetch the old man, who hated turtles because his dog,

Jake, had lost part of a leg to one of them, and who welcomed any excuse to shoot at them with his rifle. Peter often found himself wondering what became of the frogs that he and David impaled on their hooks by the rear leg, for the frogs almost always came off the hooks and disappeared after the bass had struck at them. Then, one day in August, he noticed that many of the frogs in the pool carried healed scars on their legs. Peter was touched by the realization that the injured creatures had swum great distances back to their cove, and for several minutes he pondered what to do about it. Finally he decided that it would be unfair to subject any of these brave frogs to double jeopardy, and that henceforth only unscarred frogs should be used for bait. David agreed, and the two brothers went at once to the pumping station to tell the old man of their decision.

The pumping station was a small brick building surrounded by evergreen trees and shrubs. It almost looked like somebody's house until you drew close and heard the racket and rumble of the machinery inside. The old man usually sat in a wooden chair just inside the doorway, dozing in spite of the terrible clatter, and, as always, Peter had to shout to waken him. When the old man woke up, he smiled at the boys and came outside. He was a very pale old man, with watery blue eyes and a gray stubble of beard. Now, blinking his eyes in the sunlight, he listened as Peter told him of the injured frogs that had swum back to their pool all summer long.

"Sure, and what's so strange about that?" he asked with a laugh. "If you fell and cut your leg, where would *you* go?"

"Home," David replied quickly. "I'd run home and tell my mother to put a bandage on it."

"There you are," said the old man. "Just like a little frog."

"Maybe we shouldn't hurt those little frogs," David said.

"Then what'll you use for bass bait?"

"We'll use worms," David replied.

"Or crickets," Peter said.

The old man shook his head. "Big bass like frogs," he declared. "They like something they can sink their teeth into. Why, there's only one thing they like *better* than a frog."

"What's that?" Peter asked.

"A mouse."

"A mouse!" David exclaimed.

"Yes, sir," the old man said, nodding his head for emphasis. "Catch yourself a nice field mouse, and tie him to your hook with some thread. Then put him on a shingle, let him float out over one of those deep spots where the bass hide, and yank him off. Before that mouse has swum five feet for shore, I guarantee you'll see the biggest bass you ever saw." The old man made a long, curving sweep with his forearm to signify the upward rush of the biggest bass in Hiram's Pond.

Peter and David laughed with delight as they imagined a big bass opening its jaws to swallow a helplessly trussed field mouse. But a moment later David shook his head and, frowning, announced that he would prefer to continue using frogs.

"Well, at least you don't have to feel sorry for them,"

the old man replied. "Frogs can hardly feel a thing."

"Are you sure?" David asked.

"They're cold-blooded is why," the old man said. "Fish and frogs are cold-blooded creatures. They're not like us."

"How about turtles?" Peter asked.

It was a sly question, because he knew the old man hated turtles. But the boys loved to hear the story of how Jake had lost part of his leg, and since the merest mention of turtles always evoked the story, they sat now on the grass beside the pumping station and waited for the old man to begin.

As usual, the old man commenced by calling his dog out from the pumping station. Jake was an old dog—as old for a dog as the old man was old for a man—and he came limping into the sunlight, wagging his tail, and crouched at the feet of his master. The old man bent down and lifted the dog's rear leg to show the boys where it had been severed at the lowest joint. "Look at that," he said softly. "Just like a meat cleaver had done it." The old man straightened up and pointed to the cove in front of the pumping station, where his skiff was tied to shore. "It happened five years ago—right out there," he went on. "Old Jakey was pretty old even then, but he loved to chase sunfish from those nests they build in shallow water, and he used to be wading out there all the time. Then, one day, while I was sitting inside the station, I heard this God-awful howling. I ran outside, of course, but all I could see was some terrible splashing near the boat. When I got down there, I found poor old Jake trying to make the shore. At first I couldn't make out what had got hold of him. I even thought it might be a muskrat trap someone had left in the water. Then, down below the lily pads, I saw this awful monster of a snapping turtle." The old man said this in a hushed voice, and, bringing his fingers together over his head, made an immense circle with his arms. "This big he was and he had poor old Jakey's hind paw in his jaws. He was backing out toward the deep water, and old Jake was howling for me to come help him, and trying to keep his nose above the surface. Ah, boys, it was the most awful thing I ever saw."

"What'd you do?" David asked.

"What could I do?" the old man said. "I didn't have my twenty-two in those days, so all I could do was jump into the skiff, grab old Jake by the collar, and hold on for dear life. That turtle, boys—I swear to you—was so strong he was pulling Jake and me and the skiff out through the lily pads. In the end he bit clear through the dog's leg, and that was that. I put Jake into the pickup truck and drove him over to Doc Barnes's place, and he put a tourniquet around the dog's leg and saved his life. But nobody's ever seen old Jake anywhere near the water since then. No, sir, this dog hasn't been within fifty yards of the pond in the past five years."

"What d'you think happened to that turtle?" Peter asked.

"Why, nothing happened to him!" the old man exclaimed in rage. "Nothing happened to him except he ate my poor dog's paw. He's still out there, that turtle, lurking like a reptile. They're reptiles, did you know that? Yes, sir, a turtle is nothing more than a carnivorous reptile, and that one that caught hold of poor Jake must weigh thirty pounds. Why, if a turtle that size could latch on to the ankle of a little boy like your brother here, he might even be able to drag him under."

At this point Peter laughed at David, who had begun to shiver; then he asked, "Could that turtle upset the skiff?"

The old man shook his head. "If I thought so, I wouldn't let you boys use it," he said. "But turtles are cowardly, you see. They're the most cowardly creatures I know of. They just lie in ambush like crocodiles, which are reptiles, too. Did I ever tell you boys that turtles are some of the oldest living creatures known to man? It's the honest truth. I read someplace that turtles are just as they were two hundred million years ago, when the earth was crawling with dinosaurs."

The old man breathed heavily through his nose, and turned to glare at the pond. Then he shut his dog inside the pumping station and brought out a rusty .22-caliber rifle. "C'mon, boys," he said. "We've got to keep those turtles down or they'll ruin the fishing for you."

The old man led the way to his skiff, climbed inside, and positioned himself in the bow; David got in after him and sat in the center seat; and Peter, standing in the stern, pushed off from shore with an oar. For several minutes they glided through the lily pads while the old man, who had hunched himself up in the prow, leaned the barrel of his rifle on a gunwale and studied the shore-line. Then the rifle barked, and the boys watched breathlessly as a small spotted turtle flopped off a log and disappeared beneath the surface. For the next half hour they proceeded slowly along the shore toward the southern end of the pond, and every so often the stillness was punctuated by the old man's rifle. Sometimes the bullets hit their mark, but more often than not the old man muttered in disappointment because they glanced harmlessly off the turtles' shells. "You've got to hit turtles in the head," he kept saying. "And when you see a really big turtle, you have to aim for his eye—just like when you're hunting crocodiles—or else the bullets don't do any more harm than they would to armor plate."

"Have you ever hunted for crocodiles?" David whispered.

"Nope, but I've read a lot about it," the old man replied.

"Why don't we ever see any really big turtles?" Peter asked.

"Because they're too smart to get caught out in the open," the old man said. "The only way to attract big turtles is to put out bait for them at night."

"Have you ever done that?"

"I tried it after old Jakey lost his paw, but I didn't have much luck," the old man said. "I've seen it done, though. Years ago there used to be a fellow come down here who unted turtles for the market. Yes, sir, believe it or not, some people *eat* turtles. They make soup from them. This fellow used to catch snappers here in Hiram's Pond and sell them to a hotel man up in Boston, and he made pretty good money doing it. He once told me that a dozen good-sized snappers brought fifty dollars."

"Fifty dollars!" David said. "We could buy a boat for fifty dollars."

They had returned to the mooring, and now, as they climbed out of the skiff and started across the grass toward the pumping station, both boys were thinking of the boat they could buy with fifty dollars and glancing hopefully at the old man, who was squinting down the barrel of his rifle.

When they reached the station, the old man leaned the rifle against the wall and filled a corncob pipe. Then he lighted it, puffed a long, deep puff, and sent a plume of blue smoke into the air. Finally he smiled at Peter and David. "If you wanted to catch a big snapping turtle, how would you go about it?" he asked.

"I'd use a cod line," Peter answered.

"A cod line," the old man repeated, still smiling. "And what else?"

"A hook," David said helpfully.

"What kind of a hook?"

"The same kind we use for bass."

"And what about bait?"

"A big bullfrog," Peter said.

"No, not a bullfrog," David protested. "Not for turtles."

"Let me tell you something," the old man said. "You'd never catch a really big turtle that way. In the first place, a really big turtle would cut through cod line with his jaws easier than that monster cut off poor old Jakey's paw. In the second place, even if he didn't cut the cod line, he'd straighten out the hook. Why, a big turtle could straighten out one of those little bass hooks the way I could bend a coat hanger! And in the third place, if you want to attract a giant turtle, you really have to give him something to eat. Well, how about it? Shall we try our luck?"

The two boys sat down on the grass again and, nodding in unison, waited for the old man to continue.

For several moments, however, the old man contented himself with puffing on his corncob pipe; then he leaned his shoulder against the wall of the pumping station. "Here's what we're going to do," he said. "Tonight, when I shut up the station, I'll drive into town to the hardware store and buy thirty yards of thin steel wire. Then I'll drop by the tackle shop and get us a heavy-shank hook. Meanwhile, you fellows dig some worms and catch a whole batch of sunfish. We'll need at least half a dozen, and maybe more. Put the sunfish in a basket and leave them by the door here—it doesn't matter if they get a little ripe—and tomorrow we'll set out our first trap."

Peter and David scarcely slept that night. In the morning they were up at dawn and were waiting beside the pumping station when the old man came to work in his pickup truck.

"Did you get the wire and the big hook?" Peter asked.

The old man grinned. "Did you catch enough sunfish?" he said.

"Yes!" David shouted. "We got a dozen of them."

The old man climbed out of the truck, pulled a paper bag from beneath the seat, and withdrew a long coil of steel wire and a huge hook. It was by far the largest hook that either Peter or David had ever seen, and for some moments they admired it, testing its point with the tips of their fingers.

The old man went into the pumping station to check the machinery, and when he came out, he and the boys climbed into the pickup and started over a rutted road that led along the edge of the pond. "We're going to have to find a place where we can set our trap," the old man told them. "It'll have to be someplace where we can drive the truck close to the water."

"Why do we need the truck?" Peter asked.

The old man smiled mysteriously. "You'll see," he said.

About three hundred yards from the pumping station, the old man pulled up by a clump of birch trees growing beside the water. Then he and the boys climbed out of the truck and walked to the shore. The old man threaded one end of the steel wire through the eye of the hook, and, using a pair of pliers, wrapped the excess half a dozen times around itself. Afterward he took several sunfish and threaded them on the hook until the shank was lost from sight and the sharp point was covered. Now, unrolling the rest of the wire, he whirled the hook and its heavy load of sunfish around his head, and flung it out into the water, where it sank. Then he wrapped the loose end of the wire several times around the trunk of the thickest birch tree.

"How long will we have to wait?" asked David, hunkering down on his haunches, Indian-style.

The old man chuckled softly. "All night," he replied. "Now, don't you boys disturb this wire until morning. Go bass fishing all you want and use the skiff, but stay away from this part of the pond. If we're going to catch a really big snapping turtle, we'll have to be very patient. Tomorrow morning, when you come down here, take a look at the wire. If it's still loose and sagging, pull it in, go catch some more sunfish, and I'll rebait the hook. If it's tight and won't budge, come and get me right away because that'll mean we've caught something."

"Can't we wait here if we're quiet?" Peter asked.

"Sure," the old man said, "but you'll be wasting your time. Big turtles only feed at night."

In spite of what the old man said, neither Peter nor David could bear to stay away from the steel wire that stretched out into the murky waters of Hiram's Pond. They tried a little bass fishing to pass the time, but the turtle trap was all they really thought about, and every half hour or so they tiptoed down to the clump of birch trees to see if anything had happened. Nothing had, however, and when evening came, they reluctantly said good-bye to the old man through the doorway of the pumping station, and then pedaled home on their bicycles.

In the morning they arrived at the pond even earlier than on the previous day, but they were bitterly disappointed to find the wire still sagging in the same old way. When they pulled it in, however, they were somewhat heartened to see that parts of the sunfish had been eaten away. For this reason they immediately set about catching more sunfish, and by the time the old man arrived at the station in his pickup, they were waiting for him with a fresh batch.

When the old man examined the half-eaten sunfish on the hook, he shook his head with disgust. "Those little spotted turtles just nibble away forever," he muttered. "This is what happened when I set out a line after Jakey lost his paw." The old man threaded half a dozen more sunfish on the hook, and, whirling it around his head again, tossed it out into the water; then he went off to-

ward the pumping station. "We'll try it here for the rest
of the week," he told the boys. "If we don't have any
luck by then, we'll have to find a new spot."

For the rest of the morning the boys continued to lurk
in the vicinity of the birch clump, but by afternoon they
were bored with waiting and went off to the frog pool. As
usual, they had little trouble catching frogs, but some of
the old enthusiasm had gone out of the sport. David was
especially solemn.

"Maybe we shouldn't use frogs at all," he said to Peter.
"I mean maybe we should let them stay with their fami-
lies."

Peter shook his head. "It's all right as long as we don't
use the same ones twice," he replied. "That way they
can't be too frightened because they won't know what to
expect."

David agreed that this must be so, and, happily forgetting what terror they might be engendering in the frog
population of Hiram's Pond, the two boys went out in
the skiff and spent the remainder of the afternoon fishing
for bass.

On the second day the pattern of the first repeated itself, except that after the old man rebaited the hook, the
boys went off and built fluttermills to put in a tiny stream
that ran out of the southern end of the pond.

But on the third day, when they arrived at the clump
of birch trees, they found the steel wire stretched tight
over the water. There was not the slightest bit of slack in
the wire, and when Peter noticed that the anchor loop had
bitten into the tough bark of the tree to which it had been
fastened, he nearly fell into the water with excitement.

35

Then, holding on to the trunk of the birch, and admonishing David to keep a tight grip on his waist, he tried pulling at the wire. But the wire might just as well have been encased in concrete. It not only refused to budge, it even gave a ping like a piano string when Peter struck it with his fishing pole.

"Can you see anything?" David asked, tightening his hold on his brother's waist, and peering out around him.

Peter studied the dark water beneath the lily pads, and shook his head. "It's probably just stuck on a log," he said.

When the boys reported their findings to the old man, however, he jumped up from his chair, hurried out of the pumping station, and drove his truck down to the clump of birches. After testing the wire, he shook his head solemnly. "There's something on the end of that wire, all right," he said, "and I'm willing to bet right here and now it's the biggest turtle you fellows ever saw."

"Golly," Peter said. "Will he be dangerous?"

"As dangerous as a reptile can be," the old man said darkly. Then he unfastened the wire from the tree, and wrapped it several times around the rear bumper of his truck. "Now I want you boys to stand over there," he said, pointing to a sandbank about thirty yards away. "When I start pulling on this wire with the truck, it could snap, and I don't want you getting hurt."

Peter and David nodded obediently and ran as fast as they could for the sandbank, where, crouching down, they watched the old man get into the truck, put it in gear, and start very slowly up the road. The wire stretched taut, the truck wheels spun in the dirt ruts; but the truck began to move forward. Then, incredibly, the lily pads near the shore parted with a great threshing and thrashing, and the upper carapace of an immense turtle, whose flippers were flailing the water to a froth, came to the surface. At this point the turtle made a last desperate effort to escape and almost disappeared from sight in a cascade of spray and foam; but the old man kept steady pressure upon the struggling beast with the truck until —thrashing and twisting—it was dragged entirely out of the water and onto the grass beside the shore.

Now the old man shut off the engine of the truck, set the hand brake, and, climbing out of the cab, beckoned the boys to approach. Peter and David joined him by making a wide detour that never took them closer to the writhing turtle than they had been on the sandbank. The old man was laughing softly, and in his watery eyes there was a strange light that Peter had never seen. "Look at that ugly devil," he whispered. "Wouldn't he love to get ahold of one of us?"

The giant turtle was a horrid sight. Its great shell was bearded with algae, and dripped with slime. Its head and neck were almost as long as its tail, and each of these appendages was as long as the shell. Peter and David looked with awe at the massive, beaklike jaws that were hissing and clicking like hammers upon the shank of the big hook. The jaws were immense, with horny-plated sides and terrible cutting edges, and the mouth was pink inside and opened and shut with the same implacable force of the giant machinery in the pumping station.

Now the old man motioned the boys to follow behind him, and very slowly the three of them advanced upon

37

the beast. When they were within ten feet, the old man told them to stop, for as they had got closer, the turtle had begun a furious thrashing that tightened the wire to what seemed to be its breaking point. The jaws continued to snap a drumbeat upon the hook, and the huge flippers dug and tore at the tough sod. When the old man picked up a branch and thrust it into the awful pink mouth, the jaws snapped shut, and the branch was instantly severed.

"Well, now you see what happened to poor Jakey's paw," the old man said softly.

For several moments the old man and the two boys stood watching their captive; then the old man told the boys not to budge an inch, and started for the pumping station.

"Where are you going?" Peter cried in alarm.

"To get my rifle," the old man said. "I'm going to shoot this devil right between the eyes."

"Like a crocodile," David whispered.

"That's right," said the old man with a laugh. "Right between the eyes, like a crocodile. That'll be the end of him. Just look at that devil! Why, counting the tail, he's at least three feet long. I'll bet he weighs forty pounds."

"D'you think he's the one that ate old Jakey's paw?" Peter asked.

"I hope so," the old man answered.

"Will we be able to sell him for a lot of money?" David wanted to know.

"We'll have to see about that," the old man said. "I don't know what turtles bring these days."

"What'll we do with him after you shoot him in the eyes?"

"We'll butcher him," said the old man gleefully. "It's a tough job and we'll need sharp knives and a meat cleaver. Then we'll scrape out the shell and clean off the weeds growing on it, and let it dry in the sun. Maybe we can sell the shell, too, but even if we can't, it'll make a nice-looking birdbath."

When the old man went off toward the pumping station, Peter and David backed several steps farther away from the turtle's gaping jaws. Then they watched the old man, who had begun to run. He ran awkwardly and stiffly, with his arms falling crazily at his sides, and even when he was a good distance away they could hear the breath coming through his nose in snorts.

After the old man had disappeared from view, the turtle seemed to redouble its efforts to get free of the hook and wire which held it fast. Rearing up on its hind flippers, it stretched the wire taut again, and exposed a yellow bottom that was divided into beautifully symmetrical plates. Then, suddenly, the terrible hissing noise that came from its jaws was replaced by a hoarse bellow that sounded like a cry of agony.

When this happened, David burst into tears, and even Peter felt his eyes begin to water. Now, as David began openly to weep, Peter forced himself to look away from the turtle. But there was no escaping the sound of its desperate struggle for life, and finally he said, "Let's ask the old man not to kill it."

David shook his head and gave a sob. "He won't listen. He'll say it's the same turtle that bit off old Jakey's paw."

Peter frowned and hesitated. "Well, maybe it is," he replied.

"But the turtle can't help that," said David, weeping.

"Can he help it if he's a turtle?"

"But he's a monster turtle. He'd drag you into the water if he could!"

"Not if I don't go wading," David said.

"He might catch somebody else someday."

"We could put up signs on all the trees," David said.

"How about the money for our boat?"

"I don't care about having a boat," David said. "Isn't there some way we can let him go?"

Peter looked apprehensively at the turtle's snapping jaws, and then at the taut steel wire that stretched back to the truck. "No," he answered. "There's nothing we can do."

"Can't we cut the wire?"

"How?" Peter asked. Even as he spoke, he saw the old man trotting toward them along the roadway, carrying his rifle in his hand.

"Is he coming?" David whispered.

"Yes," Peter said quietly. "It's too late."

When the old man arrived, Peter put his arm around David's shoulders. Before his eyes stretched the waters of Hiram's Pond, but the pond no longer seemed familiar. The kingfisher was still plunging toward the surface after minnows, and a kingbird was pursuing a huge butterfly above the lily pads, but now it seemed to Peter that a whole chorus of scarred frogs was croaking in unison against the savage spectacle taking place on the grass before them. When the old man fired his rifle, Peter and David closed their eyes until the report had echoed and re-echoed and died away. Then there was a moment of perfect stillness. And then they fled.

Blue Lawns **I**n my younger and more impressionable days, I was the victim of an excruciating desire to circumvent the awkward transition from youth to manhood. Successful self-dramatization is a matter of hard creative daydreaming, which is, in turn, invariably plagiaristic; and so it happened that during a brief but poignant period in the springtime of my sophomore year at Harvard, I became hell-bent on living a pastiche of what I considered to be the most romantic novel ever written—F. Scott Fitzgerald's *The Great Gatsby*.

How I happened to choose that particular book as my motif is something I have forgotten. "Choose" is not the right word, to begin with. It would be more correct to say that I wandered into *Gatsby* with the same kind of half-wishful involvement that propelled its narrator, Nick Carraway, into the social whirl of West Egg. At any rate, as with most vicarious endeavor, mine had aspects that were superficial, and others that were—by comparison, anyway—profound. As evidence of the former, I submit a sudden addiction to that insouciant salutation "old sport," which I applied with promiscuous delight (as did Jay Gatsby himself) to friend and foe alike; and as for the deeper side of my posturing, I confess to having derived considerable satisfaction from the fact that, like the early James Gatz, I too had changed my name to conform to a deep, if somewhat imprecisely motivated, need for self-metamorphosis. (In my case, it was not a question of amending my surname and given name, but of quietly dropping the uncommon middle name by which I had always been called. When I went away to prep school at the vulnerable age of fourteen, it had suddenly seemed too bizarre for further service.) As I grew more and more immersed in *Gatsby*—and therefore more determined to see life through the eyes of its characters and in terms of its action—strange things happened; imperceptibly at first, and then with a vividness that comes only with the most extravagant conceits, I began to hear Daisy's thrilling laughter in the Yard, to pass Jordan Baker's wan and haughty face on Beacon Street, and to see all lawns as blue as Carraway saw Gatsby's.

Now, when blue lawns become an integral part of a young man's spectrum, there is no limit to what else he is capable of imagining. I think it was late winter when I first became enmeshed in *Gatsby* as a way of life, but by the time the first shells were skimming over the Charles I was so submerged in my swamp of conjuration that I even remember nodding to a small, gimlet-eyed man sitting in a Harvard Square hash house just because he corresponded to the image I carried in my head of Meyer Wolfsheim. The most prosaic surroundings were conducive to my new talent for identification. My bedroom bureau, for example, never failed to evoke my favorite passage, in which Gatsby, who is showing Nick and Daisy through his mansion, takes them into his bedroom, where the elaborate pretext upon which he has built his life suddenly confronts the wondrous reality of her presence, and where, with the compulsion of a man in crisis, he starts tossing stacks of swank shirts into a sumptuous pile of disarray that soon becomes a lush, colorful handkerchief for Daisy's compulsive tears. In those days, that was for me the most poignant scene in all literature. It affected me profoundly, especially when I gazed into the shallow, paper-lined drawer that contained my own meager supply of shirts which never came back from the local Chinese laundry fluffy with the promise of soft unfolding, but always braced with cardboard, bound with garish blue paper ribbon, and smelling of stale starch. Ah, what would I not have given to have possessed Gatsby's elaborately monogrammed shirts, not have sacrificed if only I could have been so consumed with wonder at a dream come true as to have thrown them in flamboyant offering at the feet of some unattainable girl who, realizing the agony of my soul, would then have buried her lovely head in them, sobbing out the rebirth of her love for me!

Well, I must restrain myself here, for fear I may have created the impression that my efforts to perfect an alter ego modeled on Gatsby were all that occupied me during this period. On the contrary, they were merely idle moments of pleasant speculation in a fairly busy schedule, which is to say that for the most part I functioned normally. I attended classes, studied at the library, and indulged in a suitably relaxing program of athletics. In the evenings I went over to Radcliffe, or out to Wellesley, or up to the rooms of friends for drink and conversation.

I had two close friends at that time. Steven Pratt was my literary friend, and Henry Stillwater was my rowing friend. I had planned to spend the spring vacation touring Nova Scotian boatyards with Steve, who wanted to be a writer, and who was turning out some pretty fair Hemingway imitation as a result, perhaps, of having been involved with *The Sun Also Rises* to the degree that I was with *The Great Gatsby*. At any rate, the summer before, Steve had made a pilgrimage to Pamplona and run through the streets before the bulls (and then taken up with some people) and had gone down to Madrid and come back to the States in September talking seriously but modestly about good wine, fine bulls and, of course, women. During the winter he ran into a bit of trouble with *The Sun Also Rises*, possibly because the novel was too remote in setting and theme for day-to-day daydreaming, and so he reread *To Have and Have Not*, which he found much more adaptable, and which led directly to his wanting to have a boat built in Nova Scotia. With a good boat, according to Steve, a man could always make ends meet by fishing, and if the engines were fast enough —well, who knows what other business might come up?

In spite of our friendship, I was not overly enthusiastic about going to Nova Scotia with Steve—perhaps because the fishing towns and boatyards we planned to visit did not promise drama of Fitzgeraldean proportions, and, when the opportunity came up to drive down to Miami with Henry Stillwater, it was accepted by me as quickly and casually as people were forever accepting the chance to tool into old Astoria in Gatsby's yellow roadster. There was one thing to be done before I left—a rather awkward thing, but I wanted to leave my affairs in order. I saw Steve Pratt and told him I would not be going to Nova Scotia. As it turned out, I need not have worried. Steve understood perfectly.

"Don't blame you," were his exact words. "Good town, Miami."

"Have you been there yourself?" I asked.

"Just heard about it," said Steve, whose regard for *The Sun Also Rises* had produced in him a marked tendency to omit pronoun subjects. He was a swell fellow, very intense about Hemingway, and those of us who were his friends usually found ourselves playing Bill Gorton to his Jake Barnes, so we continued like that for a while, talking abbreviated dialogue that fills up pages quickly. Then Steve went to his desk, opened a drawer, and pulled out a thick manila envelope.

"Do me a favor when you get to Miami," he said, handing me the envelope. "Return this to a friend of mine."

"You bet I will," I replied. "What's in it?"

"Long story," Steve said, and went on to tell me that the envelope contained half a dozen short stories written by a gambler named Sammy Solitaire, who was one of the people he had taken up with in Pamplona the summer before. Solitaire, it turned out, worked for a syndicate that owned a *jai alai frontón* near Miami, and had gone to Spain to recruit new players. According to Steve, he was a sullen, hard-bitten fellow—a regular tough—but

45

with an odd creative streak beneath it all. From Pamplona they had gone down to Madrid together on a spree and done some extensive drinking during which Solitaire had confided in Steve that he wanted very much to get into the "writing game." By the time Steve returned to the States, he had forgotten all about it. Then, out of the blue, Solitaire had mailed the stories to him from Miami.

"How are they?" I asked.

"The stories?" Steve said. "Terrible. Awful stories. Full of sentiment."

"Did you tell this to Solitaire?"

"Couldn't bring myself to do it. Kept remembering the fine time we had in Spain. Leave it to you to say something encouraging."

After a moment's consideration, I decided that there could be little harm in exchanging a few pleasantries with Sammy Solitaire. In fact, the whole idea of meeting him intrigued me. What could fit in better with my own scheme of things than to encounter some mysterious and shady character who, like Jay Gatsby, was obviously bent on following a grand and improbable illusion?

"All right, old sport," I told Steve Pratt. "I'll give your regards to Solitaire."

"Have a fine time in Miami," he said.

It was early one morning, several days later, that Henry Stillwater and I started nonstop for Florida in his Oldsmobile convertible. I remember that we crossed the George Washington Bridge at noon; that dusk fell over us in the red clay hills of Virginia; that dawn broke in Georgia; and that during the dark of night we traversed the whole southeast corner of the Republic. Everyone suspects himself of having performed (or helped in the performance of) at least one notable feat behind the wheel of a car, and this is the result of mine: at eleven o'clock the following morning, just twenty-three hours after crossing the Hudson, Stillwater and I were swimming at Daytona Beach. The next day we continued to a rooming house in Miami, and late the same afternoon I telephoned Sammy Solitaire.

The quality of Solitaire's voice took me by surprise. It was—and there is almost no other way to describe it—a deadly voice, a voice totally without inflection, a voice that to the whole scale of human tone was what gunmetal blue is to the spectrum of color. My friend and I should come to the *frontón* for the evening's matches, it said. There would be tickets waiting for us, and if I would come upstairs to the main office at intermission, he would be glad to see me.

The *jai alai* proved to be tremendously exciting. Stillwater and I sat at mid-court, just behind a net that protects the spectators, spellbound by the speed of the ball and the grace and agility of the players, who made incredible leaps to catch it in long, curved baskets called *cestas* that were strapped to their wrists. The *cestas* were swung in great arcs that sent the pellet ricocheting off the concrete walls of the court with the sharp crack of a projectile. After watching two or three matches, we added a new dimension to our interest by joining the murmurous, humming swarm of wagerers before the betting windows; then the intermission came and I had to keep my appointment with Sammy Solitaire.

The noise of the crowd had diminished when I reached the second floor and started down a long concrete corridor toward a door that was flanked by a pair of men wearing sports jackets which bulged noticeably and identically in the region of the heart. It was one of those corridors with the total audibility of a shooting gallery; the echo of my footsteps was slightly ominous. When I drew abreast of the two men I halted, expecting to be challenged, but they merely stared back in silence. Clearly, it was up to me to begin.

"I have an appointment," I said, "with Mr. Solitaire."

This produced a flicker of recognition in the eyes of the taller one. "What about, Jack?" he asked.

"About some short stories he has written," I replied, and then, ever so slowly, as if I were about to take a pledge, I lifted the manila envelope so that it rested across my heart.

The grimace of incredulity that appeared on the face of my interrogator brought home to me with frightening clarity how ludicrous my statement must have seemed to him. I started what I hoped would be a reassuring chuckle, but it turned out to be a kind of nervous whinny. Then I took a deep breath and prepared to launch into a more detailed and convincing explanation. A geyser of unspoken words frothed at my lips, but before I could give them sound, the second guard reached for the door handle behind him and, without taking his eyes from the envelope that was by now stitched to my chest like the bull's-eye of a target, opened it just a crack and spoke to someone stationed on the other side.

"Kid here claims he's brought the boss some . . ." He paused and looked at me with disbelief.

"Short stories," I stammered.

With acute embarrassment I heard this news relayed at

a bellow throughout the room beyond the door. Then the door swung open and, with the jerky step of a mechanical duck, I lurched straight ahead into an immense office filled with desks, adding machines, and cigar smoke produced by a crew of tough-looking men wearing green-visored eye shades. The general impression was of an accounting firm except for the fact that on the desks, in neat stacks bound with thick rubber bands, was more money than I had ever seen. Why, there was enough money in that room for Meyer Wolfsheim to have fixed the 1919 World Series ten times over!

At this point a squat little fellow with a thoroughly squashed nose bounded off a stool in the far corner of the room and shuffled toward me. "So you're the editor!" he cried.

"Well, not exactly—" I began.

"I am Louis," he continued. "Much as I hate to tell you, Mr. Solitaire has had to go out to the Beach on business of the utmost possible urgence, but not ten minutes previous to your timely arrival has he called me, and this is what he has said. 'Louis,' he has said, 'transmit my apologies to the editor, assure him of my eminent arrival, and spare nothing by the meanwhile to see that he enjoys every hospitable comfort.' "

"Why, thank you," I replied, touched by this elaborate excuse that Louis had delivered with his eyes tightly shut, like a schoolboy laboring through a carefully memorized recitation.

"So siddown," said Louis, vacating the nearest chair by tapping its occupant on the nape of the neck with the edge of his palm.

I sat, and Louis sat opposite me, and there followed a

rather painful silence during which each of us conducted minute examinations of the room.

Finally Louis said, "Know Mr. Solitaire pretty good, do you?"

"As a matter of fact, I've never met him."

Louis beamed. "A real genius!" he exclaimed. "A man with great powers of brain. Let me tell you, it's an uplift just to be associated with him."

"I can well imagine," I murmured.

For a moment Louis stared reflectively at the ceiling; then he went on, "If only the boss could devote himself full-time to the kind of work you represent, why, there's no telling how high he might perspire."

No sooner had I summoned up the vigorous nod of approval this remark deserved than Louis was on his feet, looking past me toward the door. By the time I gained my own feet and turned around, I found myself confronting a slender and sallowish-handsome man of about thirty-five who proffered me a hand that—with a haste just short of discourtesy—he detached from my grasp and thrust back into the pocket of an elegant blue silk suit. The face of Sammy Solitaire was more than sallow; it was a parchment mask that threatened to immobilize his lips, the movements of which were almost imperceptible as he returned my greeting. His eyes alone held life —they were large and brown and tragic—but they acknowledged me only briefly before fixing themselves on a distant point in the room, where they appeared to focus upon some scene of sorrow too immense for the heart to bear.

There was a girl with him—a modish, pouting girl who

took up a stance some distance away, feverishly twirling a transparent plastic handbag—but Solitaire made no move to introduce us. With an expression of monumental indifference, he seemed bent on absenting himself from our presence. It was a front, of course—detachment of such high order is almost always worn as camouflage—and, wondering vaguely what lay concealed behind it, I engaged him in a hopelessly one-sided conversation that gradually, and then suddenly, lapsed into total silence.

"You sure got here quick, Mr. Solitaire," said Louis helpfully. "I bet you must've done ninety on the causeway."

"Hunh!" exclaimed the girl with wide-eyed scorn. "Ninety sitting outside in the parking lot?"

With a swift glance—a turning of his head that was as incisive as the short, deft movement of the hand with which Fitzgerald's Tom Buchanan broke Myrtle Wilson's nose—Sammy Solitaire silenced her. A rather strained and awkward moment followed. Then, mercifully, someone announced from the far end of the room that Atlanta was on the telephone, and he disappeared.

The girl giggled nervously. "Hey, don't you love this place?" she asked.

"Very nice," I replied, looking politely in the direction of her gaze as if to find some attractive feature in the concrete walls. Actually, I was trying to decipher a motive for the strange bit of deception that had been exposed, but I could make no sense of it. And just then my vague preoccupations became too much for the girl to bear.

"I mean the money-for-heavens-sake!" she cried with a mixture of annoyance and ecstasy. Then, in a breathless, confidential whisper: "Hey, don't you just want to scoop it up and run?"

Sammy Solitaire had finished with Atlanta and was standing at a desk close by, smoking a cigarette and nonchalantly flipping through a stack of twenty-dollar bills.

"How long are you and your friend staying in Miami?" he asked.

"About a week," I replied.

"Well, any time you want to come back, give Louis here a ring," he said, glancing at his watch.

Everything in his tone and gesture indicated the termination of our interview. I thanked him and extended the manila envelope. "By the way, here are your stories," I said. "Steve Pratt wants me to tell you he liked them very much."

Solitaire took the envelope as if he had never seen it before. Then, with a deprecating wave of his hand, he muttered something about scribbling a few things now and again in his spare time. A second later he was studying a tally sheet of the night's receipts.

"Well, thanks again," I said, and started away.

Solitaire dropped the tally sheet, thrust his hands into his pockets, and moved quickly between me and the door. "I've never shown my stuff to anyone before," he said, a trifle aggressively. At the same time he blew a mammoth, unconcerned cloud of smoke toward the ceiling.

There was a long silence here, begging to be filled. "Well, you should keep working at it," I said heartily.

I don't know why I said that. I suppose I hoped it would provide some reaction on his part. If only he had allowed himself a look of pleasure, however slight, or even the grimace of denial that sometimes passes for modesty, I could have concluded my errand and made my departure. But there was nothing in his face—absolutely nothing—and suddenly I was angry at this ghostly detachment. I was angry and, at the same time, resolved to elicit some human response from him.

"Listen, old sport," I told him, "your stories are better than you think. Why, they're full of promise!"

When I said this, Sammy Solitaire looked at me with such profound reproach that my first instinct was to stammer out an apology. And in that instant I realized that, in a curious way, I had offended him. It had nothing to do with the lie I had told; it was that I had trampled down his fences and breached the private sanctuary of his hopelessness.

Now his mask began to fall away. With what must have been for him a supreme show of animation, he led us across the room to a large cabinet safe. There, leaning his elbow on the top, he struck a pose that was a burlesque of his old indifference, and told Louis to open it.

"Hey, won't there be a wad of money in *there*," said the girl under her breath. She had begun to spin her handbag at a furious clip—faster even than the great revolving rotor blades of the ceiling fan overhead.

Louis was crouching before the safe, his face contorted with concentration as he turned the combination dial. Finally the last tumbler clicked into place and the door swung open, revealing a pair of handled drawers that, when opened in their turn, proved to be filled with manuscript—hundreds and hundreds of pages inserted as neatly and evenly as the pages in the binding of a book.

I made a long, exaggerated whistle. "All stories?" I asked.

"All stories," said Solitaire in a voice that sounded choked and far away.

I looked at him and saw to my amazement that he was trembling on the brink of suppressed delight. He was smiling a strange smile and shielding his eyes with his hand as if to protect them from some dazzling light. Then he was laughing. "It's a crazy thing," he said. "I can't believe—when you told me they were full of promise . . ."

He was consumed with relief, and I realized all at once that everything else—his studied detachment, the reason he had let on to Louis that I was his editor, and the story he had concocted about his late arrival—had merely served to gird him against the possibility of disappointment. Having dreamed his dream so long in private, even the *idea* of exposing it must have filled him with unbearable torment. Now he was laughing almost uncontrollably, and for a moment it appeared that he would not be able to master himself. Then, recovering, he did an incredible thing—something that has infinitely stretched the limits of my capacity for awe, and against which I have always measured subsequent marvels. He reached into the drawer, took out a whole sheaf of manuscripts, and began tossing them one by one on the floor before us—manuscripts of translucent onionskin, crisp parchment bond, and soft linen, which lost their clips and drifted leaflike as they fell. While we watched, transfixed, he pulled out more, scattering them with abandon, as if consumed with unreasoning joy at the sudden tangibility of a dream, until the white and buff and yellow pages covered the tops of our shoes in a thickening pile that rippled delicately in the currents wafted by the fan above our heads. I looked at the girl, half-expecting her, I suppose, to begin weeping, like Daisy, but she was staring openmouthed at him, her face rigid with surprise, as if he had just killed a man.

For a moment I tried to think of something to say, but of course there was nothing to say, and Solitaire would not have heard me, anyway. I doubt if he even realized we were there. When I turned at the doorway and looked back, his face was still wreathed with that strange, ecstatic expression, and the snow flurry of stories showed no signs of abating.

The last match of the evening was in progress when I rejoined Henry Stillwater, but I was scarcely aware of the shouts and applause of the crowd. Suddenly I found myself afflicted with the kind of dizziness that besets a man who has just walked out of the cinema into the strong light of day. I wanted to tell Stillwater what had happened, but he was pounding me on the back and waving six twenty-dollar bills in my face—the proceeds of a winning *quinella* ticket—and all at once the elusive fragment of wonder that I wished to communicate to him became too complicated for the mere precision of speech. So I remained silent, shutting my eyes in an attempt to keep in focus the vision I had so long and carefully nurtured, and which so unaccountably had come true. But it was already becoming blurred and slipping past me. In that room upstairs I had attained the very apotheosis of the phase I had been living—that phase when we soar

55

on in flights of incredible fancy, straws in the wind, carried back into the illusions of the past. But it was, after all, just a phase. One cannot live forever by seeking to find coincidence between life as it is and as others have seen it; and so, shortly thereafter, I closed out my youthful fascination for *The Great Gatsby*.

Yet our dreams die slowly and nostalgia remains forever.

That night, armed with the confidence of money easily acquired, Stillwater and I met two girls at a Mexican restaurant out by the airport. I believe that mine came from Ohio, but I have forgotten her name and I have only the vaguest recollection of what she looked like. All I remember is that after dinner the four of us drove out across the causeway to Key Biscayne. The convertible top was down, the air was soft, and there was a strange light gleaming on the water of the bay. The radio was playing very low, and the music had a familiar lilt.

"Make it louder, old sport," I said to Stillwater, and suddenly the girl rested her head on my shoulder and tilted her face toward mine.

" 'Old sport,' " she said with a funny little laugh. "What a crazy thing to call somebody."

I thought I would choke with joy. How thrilling her laughter was! How careless that face against my shoulder! How wan! When Stillwater turned up the volume of the radio, I recognized the George Shearing quintet picking its way through a nimble rendition of "Moon over Miami."

So I looked up at the night sky and, of course, there was.

The Secret T

he matter-of-fact manner in which Jason Marsh learned that his father had a son by a previous marriage served to temper his surprise at the discovery. One night, during his senior year at Harvard, he went to a Christmas dance at a junior college near Boston, where he was introduced to an elderly chaperon who, upon hearing his name, simply told him that he had his father's eyes, and that he resembled his older brother, John. There was no reason for Jason to doubt her because, speaking slowly enough to allow him time to trace the tenuous trail that linked them together, she went on to say that she was the sister of the man his father's first wife had later married.

Though he accepted the existence of an older brother, Jason naturally reviewed what he knew of the chronology of his father's life, beginning (of course) with himself and working backward. He had been born in 1932; his father and mother had been married in 1930; and twelve years before that his father had served with the American Expeditionary Force in France. The years between 1919 and 1930 were, however, a blank as far as Jason was concerned. As a boy he had asked his father to tell him about the Great War, in which his father had lost part of a kneecap to a shell fragment, and as a young man he had questioned his father about the Great Depression, in which his father had lost their first house to a bank. But he had never entertained any particular curiosity about the intervening years; nor had his father, who was an architect, ever volunteered much information about them, except for an occasional reference to his professional life. Jason remembered his father's saying that he had been associated with an architectural firm that had failed a few years after the crash. Jason also remembered his pointing out a building on Tremont Street where he had had his first office. Jason racked his brains to remember anything else that might be pertinent, but without success. In the end he was merely able to establish the elderly chaperon's revelation as a historical possibility, which was all the more frustrating because he had begun by acknowledging it as a fact.

Jason's parents and his young sister, Jean, lived in a suburb of Boston. When Jason went home for Christmas vacation a few days after his discovery, he found them happy over the unexpected news that his brother Arthur, who was a freshman at Stanford, had decided to fly east for the holidays. A family reunion took place the following evening in the terminal building at Logan Airport. Then the five of them drove into the downtown section of the city and ate supper at a Chinese restaurant on Joy

Street which they had been patronizing since Jason could remember. After supper his father stopped to pay the bill and chat with the proprietor, an old man with hooded eyes who wore a pair of tiny glasses with thick lenses and who sat upon a high stool fingering an abacus. Each time Jason had gone to the restaurant as a child, the old man had written his name for him in Chinese, using a brush and ink and fashioning the graceful, lilting characters with swift, sure strokes. Jason had treasured the scraps of paper for a long time until, coming upon them in his desk one day and placing them side by side, he noticed with disappointment that each time the old man had written his name, he had done it differently. Now Jason smiled at the old man and heard his father remind him that he had been coming there for thirty years.

"I lemember!" said the old man, laughing and pointing a finger at Jason. "Little boy all glown up."

"Yes, indeed," said Jason's father. "Good night."

"All glown up!" the old man shouted gleefully as they went out the door. "Good night! Good night!"

It was snowing outside. The neon lights of the restaurants were reflected in the flakes, and behind the swirling screen the statuettes and figurines that filled the windows of the shops in Chinatown seemed to shimmer. As he walked through the snow with his father, Jason remembered that when he and his brother and sister were children, the family dinners in Chinatown had always ended with a visit to one of the shops, where each of them was allowed to purchase a tiny porcelain animal. Now a whole parade of fragile horses, elephants, turtles, and dragons (which they had endlessly traded and bickered over and

59

which had long since broken into fragments and disappeared) passed before him. For a moment he thought of reminding his father of the animals, but he was suddenly shy of evoking the past. The thirty years that his father had recalled for the Chinese proprietor did not seem so much a span of time as a jumble of possibilities which tumbled through his head with the turbulence and disorder of the falling snow. And as for that myopic old man who had never written his name the same way twice— which little boy did he claim to remember?

On the drive home Jason sat up front with his father, who peered intently through the windshield, steering the car over the slippery roads as if he were guiding a ship through dangerous shoals. His mother, sister, and brother sat in back talking about California, but Jason heard only echoes of the conversation. He was thinking that his mother must surely share the secret with his father and that they had decided upon silence together. He could scarcely believe that Jean and Arthur knew, but, considering the circumstances of his own discovery, it seemed probable that sooner or later they would also chance upon the knowledge of their father's earlier marriage. Did his father really believe that his secret could be kept from them forever? Jason wondered whether his father were ever tempted—especially now that they were grown—to take them into his confidence. (As it was, the fact that he had not done so was far more disturbing to Jason than the fact that he had previously been married and had another son.) For a moment Jason considered whether he should assume the responsibility his father was avoiding and take it upon himself to tell Arthur and Jean. But suppose there were other reasons for his father's silence? Jason glanced at his father's grimly intent profile and wondered whether he ever saw his other son, and if he did not, why? The questions tugged at Jason's spirit. They isolated him. In this mood, his father's secret weighed upon him with heavy disproportion.

When they pulled into their driveway, he awoke as if from sleep, startled to find that they were still together within the confines of the car, and that he could discern the familiar outline of the house and the doors of the garage beneath it.

His father turned around, triumphant and beaming. "Well, here we are!" he cried. "Home for Christmas."

While Jason's mother, brother, and sister went into the house, Jason opened the garage doors so that his father could put away the car. As it moved slowly past him, he saw his father's face faintly illuminated by the light of the dashboard, which showed, however, only the barest outline of his features, leaving all the rest without substance in transparent shadow, to be imagined. Now his father switched off the headlights and the garage became dark and cavernous again. In the moment of silence that followed, Jason found himself wondering whether, at this time of year, his father must not be thinking of his other, oldest son.

On New Year's Day, Jason went ice fishing with his father and brother on the Concord River. It was a traditional outing that—weather and ice permitting—they undertook each year. The river was covered with frozen snow, and because of a ridge of ice chunks that had been heaved along either bank by the pressure of the current, it looked like a highway winding between the wooded hills. The part they fished was at a bend about half a mile upstream from an old plank-and-girder bridge, and to reach it they walked close to the bank in single file. Jason's father went first, occasionally testing the ice for soft spots with the blade of a long, wood-handled chisel; Arthur followed in his footsteps and Jason came last, pulling a box sled that held a dozen tip-up trays, a bucketful of minnows, and their lunch. When they arrived at the bend, they chopped holes in the ice and set out the tip-ups in three clusters that were approximately a hundred yards apart, forming a triangular pattern within the arc of the river bend. Then they separated to tend them.

When Jason got back to his set of traps, he pulled in each of his lines to see whether the hooks were still baited, and lowered them into the river again. Looking across the ice, he saw that his father and brother were also examining their lines. For some moments he watched their slow progress from one trap to the next, struck by the profound solitude in which each of them performed his separate tasks. Only the river ice, groaning sporadic protest against contraction, and the planks of the old bridge which rumbled with the passage of an occasional vehicle made sounds to break the stillness. When his father lit his pipe, Jason saw a cloud of blue smoke hover in the chill, wintry air, rise slowly above the frozen river and the bleak, wooded hills, and then flee upward into the pale sky—dissolving, disappearing, gone.

Suddenly, filled with a sense of their fantastic visibility against the expanse of snow and ice, he imagined that he was looking down from a great height upon his father, his brother, and himself. He found himself thinking that even if the ice should give way beneath them, dropping them into the dark current, there would still be his older brother; but he could not endure the loneliness that accompanied this vision, and now he forced it from his mind by riveting his gaze upon his father. My father is only a hundred yards away, he told himself. I will cross over and tell him what I have learned. I will say, "Father, I know about my older brother." There will be a look of surprise and relief upon my father's face when I say this, Jason thought. He may even smile. Then he will tell me all about it. He will probably end by saying, "Jason, this doesn't make any difference between us, you know," and I will say, "I know it doesn't, Father, but I'm glad you told me, and I hope you'll tell Arthur and Jean someday." Then we'll shake hands and wish each other a happy New Year, and on my way back I'll stop by to visit Arthur, and perhaps we'll be lucky and catch some fish before the day is through. . . .

Jason started across the ice toward his father, who waved a greeting. But before he had gone halfway, there was a shout from Arthur, and, turning, he saw his younger brother running toward a trap whose red flag, suddenly unsprung, was dancing above the snow. Now both Jason and his father hurried toward Arthur, converging upon him even as, hauling in line hand over hand, he pulled a large fish through the hole. It was a long, sleek pickerel with brilliant green chain markings on its sides and a white belly. Jason looked down at the pickerel flopping on the ice, and his father grasped each of his sons around the shoulders, hugging them to him with elation.

"We're going to have a big pickerel supper," he declared.

"You always say that," Arthur protested.

"You'll see—by tonight we'll have enough pickerel for a regular feast!" his father replied. For a moment longer he held his sons tightly in his grip; then, releasing them, he hurried back across the ice to his traps.

Jason watched him go, wondering whether he should follow, but his earlier sense of isolation had been diminished by his father's embrace, and he decided against it. Instead he returned to his own traps, and once again the three of them took up separate stations on the winding expanse of ice and snow. At this point Jason found himself strangely relieved that he had not confronted his father with the secret. The secret had been kept too long and therefore possessed too much history and continuity of its own to be broached except at the right moment. Besides, was it not far better to wait until his father broached it himself? Surely one day he would feel bound to do so, Jason told himself. Now, looking down at one of the holes in the ice, he noticed that during his absence a skim incorporating tiny particles of snow and slush had formed and was congealing in faint wrinkles before his eyes. Tonight, he knew, the temperature would drop, and by morning the holes would be frozen solid. Thus did the river keep its winter silence.

Once Jason had decided to wait for his father to tell him the secret of his own accord, he ceased to think about it. After his graduation he was inducted into the

army and shipped to Germany, and in the months that
followed the secret remained dormant within him as if it
were some kind of hibernating animal. Except for his
mother, who wrote to him regularly, the Marshes were not
a corresponding family, but in the spring of Jason's second year in Europe his father suffered a heart attack.
During the month he was recuperating at the Massachu-
setts General, there was a flurry of letters from everyone.
There was even a full-page letter from his father, who almost never wrote letters of any kind. "I'm sixty-four,
Jason, and they tell me this kind of thing is not uncommon at my age," his father wrote. "The doctors say I've
made a good recovery, though, and I'm going to do what
they advise and take things easy, so don't worry."

Jason was greatly relieved to hear from his father, but
he was worried. When his sister wrote that she had been
accepted at the University of Geneva and would be coming through Paris, in June, he was delighted at the prospect of hearing some firsthand news. He went to Paris
on a three-day pass, met his sister, and took her to lunch
at a restaurant on the Ile Saint-Louis. Afterward they
went walking along the Seine. Jean said that their father
was in good spirits and that he had gone back to work.

"He seems much more relaxed," she went on. "He
doesn't worry about things the way he used to." She
paused and smiled at Jason. "I think he misses you a lot,
Jason—I mean having you around to confide in."

"Funny you should say that," Jason replied with the
trace of a smile. "When he was in the hospital and I was
hoping he would be all right and wouldn't die, I was also
hoping that he would live to tell us something he probably

should have told us years ago."

"You mean that he was married before and has another son?"

"Then he did tell you," Jason said.

"No, I've known about it a long time," his sister replied; "ever since I was a little girl." Now, seeing amazement on Jason's face, she tossed her hair and laughed. "I woke up one summer night during the war and heard him talking to Mother about it," she went on. "He was terribly upset, which is why I remembered even though I didn't really comprehend all of what they were saying until much later, when I'd spoken to Aunt Louise. Evidently Daddy had heard from his other son for the first time in many years. His son was at Fort Devens and was about to go overseas. He called Daddy up and they made a dinner date for that night, but the boy never came."

"Maybe he couldn't get a pass," Jason said. "Maybe he got shipped out."

His sister shrugged. "I don't know," she replied. "Aunt Louise didn't either."

They were midway across one of the bridges and had stopped to look down upon some fishermen on a quai. "When did you talk to Aunt Louise?" Jason asked.

"One of those times she came east," his sister said. "She was guarded, of course, because she knew I'd found out accidentally, but she told me that Daddy hadn't seen his other son for nearly twenty years. She said he had seen him regularly up until the time he was ten years old, but that just after Arthur was born, his first wife remarried and went to live in Oregon. She said the divorce was bitter—not an amicable settlement, as the saying goes—so there was no correspondence. Also it was the middle

of the Depression. Daddy's firm failed and the bank fore-
closed on the Lexington house. When he couldn't keep
up payments on the car, he lost that too. Then I came
along and—well, according to Aunt Louise, Daddy didn't
have much choice. His attention had to be with all of us."

Jason found himself assessing what his sister had told
him in the context of how the secret had unfolded for
each of them. For some time the incongruity between the
various places of disclosure—their home, the junior college, a Boston restaurant, and this bridge above the Seine
—blurred his ability to understand. "Did it bother you
very much?" he asked finally. "Knowing?"

"No, I don't think so. I just accepted it, I guess."

"Perhaps we ought to tell Arthur," Jason said.

"Arthur!" his sister exclaimed. "Why, Arthur's known
about it almost as long as I have. I think one of our cous-
ins told him."

"But that's impossible!" Jason protested. "I mean
Arthur would have told me."

"Would he?"

Jason looked at his sister's face and saw laughter lurking in her eyes. "That's right," he said slowly. "You
didn't."

"We were happy children," his sister replied. "Why
bring up something that might have disturbed us? Father
and Mother must have decided there was no point in telling us when we were young. Then, with one thing and another, but mostly time, it no longer became a question of
not telling us or of withholding something but rather of
simply going on the way we always had. Do you know
what I mean?"

"Yes, I suppose so," Jason replied. "I suppose it got

to be a question of continuity."

"Poor Daddy. Perhaps it's still too painful for him."

"That's something we may never know," Jason said. "That's a subsidiary secret. One begets another."

After this meeting with his sister, nearly eight years went by before Jason spoke of the secret again. By this time Jason had become a lawyer, was married, had a son of his own, and was working for a New York law firm. His father was in semiretirement, and at Christmastime his mother flew to Washington to spend several days with Jean, who was a secretary in the State Department. Jason invited his father to spend the holiday in New York; it was a pleasant visit but a short one. His father was design-ing a summer house for an old friend and wanted to get back to work on it, so the day after Christmas—a cold, blustery morning—Jason accompanied him to Grand Central Station. His father bought a Pullman seat on the three-o'clock train to Boston. Then, after checking his father's bag and agreeing to meet at the information booth fifteen minutes before departure time, the two men sepa-rated—Jason going off to his office and his father to some art galleries on Fifty-seventh Street.

At the appointed time Jason arrived at the information booth and saw his father approaching from the far end of the concourse. Tall, white-haired, and elegant-looking in a black coat, his father walked slowly, using a cane. But as he drew closer Jason noticed that his gait, which had slackened perceptibly in the years following his heart attack, was dissolving into a shuffle as he came across the marble floor, and that his face had, since morning, become ashen and gray. When his father reached the booth, he leaned an elbow on the circular counter, smiled wanly at Jason, and, seeing the concern in his son's face, shook his head.

"I'm okay," he said ruefully. "I just walked too far against the wind."

"D'you want to sit down?" Jason asked.

"No, but I think I'll rest a moment."

Jason watched his father unbutton his overcoat, reach into his vest pocket, and take out a small silver box containing his nitroglycerin pills. Then, with the shyness of a boy stealing candy, his father slid back the lid of the box with his thumb, withdrew one of the tiny pills, and slipped it beneath his tongue. A moment later, still leaning on his elbow, he was nonchalantly examining the vast ceiling overhead.

"How are you?" Jason asked quietly.

"I'm okay," his father said again. "Stop looking at me that way."

"Sorry," Jason said. "I'm a little scared, I guess."

"Me too," his father replied, glancing at the station clock. "Let's go have a cup of coffee."

They went slowly across the concourse floor to a sandwich shop that sat against the wall of an adjoining corridor. The shop was a garish, glassed-in hodgepodge of chrome, plastic, and Formica. Jason and his father sat on adjacent stools, ordered their coffee, and for some moments sipped it in silence. Glancing sideways at his father, Jason was relieved to see that color was flowing back into his cheeks and that the tiny muscles at the corners of his mouth had relaxed. Then abruptly his father straightened up.

"Jason, there's something I've been meaning to tell you for a long time," he said. "Years ago, before I met your mother, I was married and had a son. It's a part of my life I've almost forgotten. I've had to forget it because, for one reason and another, I haven't seen my other son for nearly thirty years. I'm telling you now because I consider you my oldest son, Jason, and someday, when I'm gone, I want you to tell Arthur and Jean."

Jason found himself suddenly and acutely embarrassed, as if he had regressed to that agonizing adolescent stage where nearly every parental statement seemed to constitute an awful indiscretion. He almost felt like shrugging. Instead he thought of the day on the river years before when he had started across the ice to confront his father, but the loneliness that had animated him then was gone forever. He considered telling his father the truth—that he had known for a long time and that Arthur and Jean had known even longer—but suddenly he found himself flinching from the secret as if from a soft spot where shell ice masks a treacherous current. He had kept it too long. It had become a part of him. "I'm glad you told me, Father," he managed to say. "It doesn't matter, of course, and"—here Jason took a deep breath—"it wouldn't have even if you had told me long ago."

"I know that," his father said quietly. "I figured that if you had found out when you were younger, you would have come to me. The reason I'm leaving it up to you to tell Arthur and Jean is—well, it happened forty years ago, Jason. I'm over seventy now. I'm too old to go raking all that up again."

"Yes," Jason said. He looked at his watch and drank down the rest of his coffee. "We'd better be off," he told his father. "It's ten of three."

But a few moments later, as they went down the ramp to the track platform and walked out toward the front of the train, Jason was overcome by a profound depression. Here in this cavernous place with its infinity of gloom and darkness and its concrete pillars hanging like stalactites above some underground river; here, where the winking lantern of a trackman bobbed in the eerie distance like the light of a small boat; here, carrying an overnight bag whose lightness suddenly seemed appalling, and walking beside this aged man whom he would always love, Jason forced censure from his mind as he would have suppressed himself from cursing in a church.

At the door of the Pullman car he handed his father's bag to a porter with great reluctance, as if by relinquishing that feathery vessel he was admitting that it contained far too little of all the love, hope, and misunderstanding that had ever passed between them. He felt the silence of his father tugging at him now like his own fear of his father's death. When they reached his father's seat, the older man removed his overcoat and handed it to Jason, who folded it carefully and placed it upon the rack overhead. Then they went to the smoking section, where his father sat down and filled his pipe with tobacco.

"I had a fine time, Jason," he said. "It was a wonderful Christmas. Tell Mary how much I enjoyed it."

Jason nodded and looked down at his father, who was applying a lighted match to the tobacco in his pipe. A

71

moment later he was enveloped by a cloud of fragrant smoke that called forth familiar memories: the old house, his father's easy chair. "Ring us up when you get home tonight so we'll know you got back okay," he said.

"Take care of yourself, Jason."

"Goodbye, Father. Don't forget to call."

"Jason?"

Jason turned in the narrow passageway between the baggage shelves that flanked the doorway.

"I hope you're not bothered by what I told you," his father said. "It doesn't change anything between us, you know."

"Of course it doesn't," Jason replied.

His father had removed the pipe from his mouth. "I wonder if I was right not telling you before," he murmured.

Twice in the moment of silence that followed came the most inexorable cry that Jason thought he would ever hear—the boarding cry. Then, as the shouts died away, he found himself thinking that surely in all these years the sheer exercise of will involved in the attempt to forget and to displace had also been a curious and merciful antidote to suffering. Now he saw his father watching him, waiting.

"Sure, Father," he said softly. "You were right."

As Jason walked back across the station concourse, he glanced at the clock on top of the information booth. It was three minutes past the hour. Even now the train was pulling away from its pier, a sinister vessel, swaying gently, rocking, and then coasting easily through the

Stygian darkness. In a few minutes it would emerge from that gloom and glide, as if through a walled canal, past the tenements of Harlem to another river. There would be a whole series of rivers—the Housatonic, the Connecticut, and the Thames—and Jason breathed easier as he imagined his father looking out at them in daylight.

Now the train, gathering speed, was arrowing across Rhode Island. Night was falling and the orange windows of the coaches were flashing through the blackness with the implied continuity of the dashes that connect electrified headlines moving across dark façades. Westerly and Providence went by, and then the trip (as it had always seemed to Jason on his way home) was a breathless downhill rush. There was a brief pause at the station on Route 128, where cartops glistened as if awash, and then Back Bay. *Back Bay? Baack Bayuhh!* More rocking and swaying now, and some not so gentle shunting back and forth. Yet can the seas of a harbor be choppy on a windless night? In any case, passengers are moving toward the rail to disembark. South Station. Home.

Jason was climbing the stairway at the western end of the concourse, holding his breath and waiting for the telephone to ring, when suddenly he saw that the balustrade above was empty. How strange to find it empty— this vantage spot where he had almost always, if idly, noticed people watching the floor below as attentively as the mindless sentinels who position themselves on bridges over highways. Yet in spite of his previous contempt for them, he too was drawn now to the rounded marble railing as if he were some substance that nature had found handy to fill a vacuum. There, looking down upon the concourse, Jason saw hundreds of people crisscrossing every which way without discernible pattern or direction.

As he watched them, his vision of the train that was bearing forever away (even if to safety) the frail voyager who was his father faded and he found himself imagining that he and his family were part of the crowd and that they were, as everyone else seemed to be, traveling separately. The fact that each of them had harbored the secret separately and so long had not brought them closer together, nor had it put them further apart, he decided. It had simply maintained—like the stress function of the girders that filled his father's architectural blueprints; like the delicately balanced extenuations of a mobile; like the secret he was now keeping from his father—a kind of equilibrium. For a moment longer Jason continued his vigil above the concourse floor; then he turned away from that sea of singular motion and went out through the portals into the street. I'll have to write to Arthur and Jean, he told himself.

The Siphon Stephen Bradford did not consider himself a superstitious man. He readily accepted third service on matches, thought nothing of walking beneath ladders, and never rapped his knuckles on wood. On the day the water stopped flowing from the well at his weekend cottage in Connecticut, however, he experienced a tremor of foreboding, as if he were witnessing a portent. He was also surprised and disappointed—surprised because the system he had devised for bringing water from the well to the cottage had never failed during the three years that he and his wife, Linda, had been going there, and disappointed because he was proud of the system and had been looking forward to showing it to his mother and father, who were driving down from Boston on their first visit. The idea for the system had come to Stephen on a summer evening, when, carrying a bucket of water down from the well, he was reminded of an experiment he had conducted with beaker and tubing in a high-school physics class. The following morning he went out and bought several lengths of plastic garden hose, some pipe, and a faucet. After linking the lengths of hose together, he attached one end of a piece of pipe and inserted the pipe into his well, which was located on a wooded knoll above the cottage. Downhill, a hundred and fifty yards away, he ran the other end of hose into the cottage and attached it to a faucet, which he had mounted above the sink. A local plumber named Spaulding started water flowing from the well by drawing it through the pipe and hose with a small electric pump, and since then —except during winter months, when everything froze up and Stephen and Linda spent their weekends in the city —there had always been a steady flow through the siphon whenever the hose was connected and the faucet turned on.

In the course of time Stephen attached a strange and special significance to the siphon. He did this because— in spite of the fact that it had been his idea to install it— he had no real understanding of how or why a siphon operated. He knew intuitively that the excess weight of water running downhill through the hose maintained the continuous flow, but in the ten years since he had conducted the experiment in high school, he had forgotten that it was atmospheric pressure which kept forcing water up through the pipe to begin with. As a result, he considered the siphon not as a principle of physics, but as one of those mysteries of nature which somehow work. He was, however, quite content to think of it in this way. The siphon provided a sacred link with the mysterious and subterranean flow of table water that collected in his

well. It appealed to the romantic in him. It filled him
with a sense of harmony and well-being. It not only made
life in the cottage convenient, it seemed to possess the
continuity of life itself. Consequently, Stephen took pains
to protect the siphon from possible damage or accident
during his absence. On Sunday nights, before he and
Linda drove back to the city, he separated the uppermost
length of hose from the others and propped the open,
gushing end high enough in the fork of a tree so that
the water no longer bubbled forth; on Saturday mornings, when they returned, he took the hose down and,
before connecting it, waited for the water to flow again
with the mixture of awe and serene assurance that sus-
tains pilgrims who await a miracle. Never for a moment
did he envisage the possibility that the water might fail
to come. For this reason, now that it *had* failed, his initial
foreboding, surprise, and disappointment soon gave way
to a deep sense of puzzlement. Malaise engulfed him.
Doubt seeped through him. He felt alienated—cut off
like the cottage from its source of clear, cold water—and
strangely vulnerable.

For some moments Stephen stood rooted to the spot;
then, hoping to start the flow again, he sat on the ground,
placed the end of the hose in his mouth, and tried to
draw water through it by inhaling deeply. The effort
soon made him dizzy, however, and he gave up. As he
sat on the ground, trying to regain his sense of equilibrium, he decided that the well must have gone dry. He
stood up and, still feeling disoriented, followed the hose
through the undergrowth until he reached the well, which
was capped by a round wooden cover. Brushing away

some dead leaves and twigs that had collected on top of
the cover, he pulled it aside and looked down into the
well. When his eyes became accustomed to the darkness,
he could see that although the water level had dropped,
the well was still nearly one-third full. Kneeling, he
rested his elbows on the rim of the well and, bathing his
face in the coolness that rose from the dank stones into
the dry October day, studied the surface of the water. He
remained in this position for a long time, as if hopeful
that, by peering intently enough, he might dispel the
mystery of the siphon, fathom out its workings, and
understand what delicate balances of gravity and pressure had been disrupted. He reasoned that as the water
level of the well had fallen, the water in the hose must
have receded back toward the siphon pipe, but beyond
this point he was unable to pursue the problem in logical
or sequential fashion. His own reflection—altered and
made strangely minuscule by lack of light—stared back
at him from a patch of sky that was mirrored in the surface of the water, and, unaccountably, he found himself
thinking of a visit he had made to a heart specialist with
his father, in September. His father had returned from a
business trip complaining of shortness of breath. Alarmed
because his father had suffered a coronary occlusion
several years before, Stephen had driven home to Boston. The specialist, an old friend of the family, was world-
famous and respected—a man who treated Oriental
potentates and ordinary housewives with the same gentle
detachment. After the examination he came into an ante-
room where Stephen was waiting, and told him that his
father had undergone a mild cardiac crisis, but that his

heart seemed to have made a fairly good adjustment. The doctor said this very quietly and professionally; then, seeing the concern on Stephen's face, he shrugged. "Your father's heart and the arterial system surrounding it are seventy years old," he went on. "They're wearing out." The doctor had not added "Someday" as he arched his eyebrows into an additional shrug, but he might as well have. Someday, inevitably, there would be another disruption, another blockage, another crisis . . .

Stephen put the thought from his mind, got to his feet, and replaced the cover on the well. Then he started back toward the cottage. It was nearly noontime, and his father and mother were planning to arrive in time for lunch. Even now they must be turning off the Merritt Parkway, following the map he had drawn and mailed them, and starting over the road leading north and west along the Housatonic Valley. Stephen found himself imagining their progress as if he were looking down from some immense vantage point; then his vision shifted and became abstract, and he saw his father, a frail voyager, traveling slowly and laboriously through a venous maze of winding country roads. Desperately, as a floundering man seeks footage, Stephen forced himself to look at the cottage. He was glad that his father would see it in sunshine. Tiny, white, and clapboarded, the cottage sat on a high wooded ridge above the river valley, where it was dwarfed by tall trees and surrounded by stone walls—vestiges of another century when the land had been opened and farmed. Thus enclosed—pressed against by walls and diminished by woods—it tended to seem gloomy and additionally submerged on gray days. In sunlight, however, it stood out like a balcony—a balcony in the forest, Stephen was fond of thinking, where no one ever intruded upon them, and where, thrown back upon themselves, he and Linda had spent happy weekends. As he crossed the yard, he peered through the front window and saw Linda spooning lunch into the baby, who, catching sight of Stephen, began mugging for his benefit through a mouthful of cottage cheese and pineapple. Stephen mugged a face in return and did a crazy jig in the yard. But his jollity was enforced; he could not help remembering that while Linda was carrying the baby, he had often found himself hoping that his father would live to see it. How long had he been afraid of his father's death? he wondered. Now he opened the door of the cottage and went inside.

"The siphon's stopped working," he said.

Linda responded to the announcement with a frown of annoyance. (Stephen had the feeling, however, that he might as well have told her the right front tire of the car had gone flat.) Then she turned back to the baby, who, in high good humor at the sight of Stephen, was resisting the last mouthful of lunch.

"It's going to be damned inconvenient," Stephen went on. "We'll have to lug in water by the bucketful."

Intent upon the baby, Linda merely sighed and nodded.

"I could call the plumber and ask him to bring his pump," Stephen said gloomily. "But I have no idea what's wrong, and I doubt if he'll want to come all the way over on a Saturday."

"We'll just have to make do," Linda replied. She wiped the baby's mouth, untied his bib, and, gathering him up in her arms, carried him into the tiny bedroom at the

rear of the cottage for his nap. "Say sleepy-bye to
Daddy," she said.

Stephen was unnerved by her aplomb. It was not that
he expected her to understand the anxiety that had descended upon him; it was just that he was not prepared
to realize the extent to which her necessities differed
from his. Suddenly he felt terribly alone. He picked up
the telephone and dialed Mr. Spaulding's number. The
plumber's wife answered and informed him that her husband was out and would not return until late afternoon.
Stephen hung up the phone and went outside. He was
glad that Mr. Spaulding had not been at home. The idea
of the pump disturbed him; it did not seem right, somehow, to renew the flow through the siphon by artificial
means. There must be some perfectly simple and natural
way to get the siphon working again. Perhaps by lowering something bulky into the well and thus raising the
water level . . . Immersed in the possibilities of this
scheme, Stephen was hardly prepared to hear his father's car climbing up the driveway through the woods.
He was, moreover, surprised to find that even as it came
into view, his relief at seeing his father behind the wheel
was attended by a feeling of profound despair.

During the next half hour Stephen managed to put the
siphon from his mind as he showed his mother and father the cottage and its surroundings, and described the
various projects and improvements that he and Linda
had undertaken there together. The inventory was a long
one and included the cottage itself, which they had carefully calked and painted during the summer; a walk composed of flagstones they had discovered in an abandoned

quarry and set into the tough sod covering the front yard; window boxes filled with geraniums, impatience, and fuchsia, which Linda tended along with a flower bed containing peonies, petunias, parsley, and mint; a flourishing rhododendron whose roots, following a tip gleaned from the gardening section of the Sunday newspaper, they religiously sprinkled with coffee grounds; an evergreen transplanted from the depths of the forest, which, belying its name by turning a disappointing brown in December, delighted them by reviving in May; and a screen porch they had built the first year, where, safe from mosquitoes, they sat sipping rum and soda on summer evenings and listening to the last thrush calling from the woods. When Linda and Mrs. Bradford went inside to prepare lunch, Stephen took his father on a leisurely stroll through a tract of woodland from which he was clearing brush. On the way they stopped to inspect a toolshed where Stephen kept an ax, a bow saw, a shovel, a brush-cutter, a battered lawnmower, and a large old-fashioned scythe which he had bought at an auction to cut down weeds that grew along the driveway in August and September. Then they heard Linda calling them to lunch, and returned to the yard. Stephen set up a card table on the grass and brought out some chairs from the screen porch. Linda carried out a tray of sandwiches and cups of hot soup, and they all sat down. At this point Stephen's father turned to him with a strange smile on his face.

"Stephen, how'd you ever get my old scythe down here?" he asked.

"Scythe?" Stephen echoed.

"Yes, scythe," replied Mr. Bradford, chuckling as if

he had trapped his son in some childish evasion. "I'll have you know I've been missing that scythe for a long time."

Stephen's mother reached across the table and laid a hand upon his father's arm. There was amusement at the corners of her mouth and concern in her eyes. "Why, George," she said softly. "You gave that scythe away twenty-five years ago. You gave it to Malcolm Henderson when we moved to Belmont."

For a moment everyone laughed, including Stephen's father; then they began to eat. Stephen looked carefully at his father, who seemed totally unconcerned about his lapse of memory, and then at his mother and Linda, who had begun talking about the care of plants during autumn and winter. And, suddenly, he was once again overcome by depression. Was it inevitable, he wondered, that as one grew older the span of memory tended to become fragmented and blocked? The idea seemed not only inevitable but horribly ominous. Studying his father's face, Stephen found it older, leaner, and infinitely lined. The skin and flesh had tautened visibly around the eyes and mouth. Now the season intruded upon Stephen with a vengeance. The smell of decaying leaves and vegetation, already disintegrating into dust, filled his nostrils and took away his appetite. He glanced up at the bare branches of the trees and thought of them contracting and forcing the sap to withdraw into the trunks and descend toward the roots. Everything was shrinking. He sought desperately to break the spell's new onslaught. He pointed to the garden hose running across the yard beside the table and told his father what had happened to the siphon. His father listened attentively and asked several questions about the depth of the well and the water level; then, with a shake of his head, he fell silent and stared off into the woods. Stephen found himself listening to echoes of the women's conversation. His mother was telling Linda that rhododendron tended to wither in winter sun, and that the fuchsia, though it would soon turn spindly, might come back to life in the spring if allowed to go dormant in a dark place. Dormant, dying, dead—the words thumped hollowly in Stephen's spirit. His head began to throb. He looked at his father, who, having finished his lunch, seemed immersed in a dream.

"How're you feeling these days?" he asked.

"Me?" his father replied vigorously. "I'm feeling fine! I was just thinking about this siphon of yours. What d'you say we figure it out and get it running again?"

After lunch Linda and Stephen's mother drove off with the baby to do some shopping. Stephen and his father climbed the knoll to the well. The older man climbed with difficulty, even though the rise was slight, and stopped halfway to rest. How slowly he moved these days, Stephen thought. He seemed to be performing life at tempo adagio. When they reached the well, Stephen pulled away the wooden cover. His father pulled a pipe from his jacket pocket and filled it with tobacco; then, studying the well, he struck a match and applied the flame to the top of the bowl.

"Funny," he said, puffing smoke into the air. "Something like a siphon. It's elemental. Why, it's so elemental you take for granted you know all about it. So it eludes you. Exasperating, hey?"

Stephen nodded and replaced the cover on the well. "Never mind," he said morosely. "I can haul enough water for the weekend."

His father shook his head. "I'm not giving up," he declared. "I'm going inside awhile to lie down and figure the thing out."

While his father was resting, Stephen cleared brush from the woods behind the toolshed. The brush was thick and tangled and difficult to get at, but he was grateful for the chance to work because it took his mind off the siphon. When he quit, an hour or so later, he walked around the front of the cottage and found his father standing beside the garden hose.

"Listen to this!" his father said triumphantly. "When the water level of the well recedes, the water in the hose also recedes, creating a vacuum that nature, of course, fills with the nearest thing at hand—in this case a column of air. Usually, when you take the hose down from the tree, the pressure of the water is strong enough to push out the air, but this time the resistance of the air was greater. The only solution, therefore, is to draw out the air and create another vacuum that will be filled by water. In other words, the problem is exactly what it must have been when you first installed the siphon. What did you do then?"

"I had a plumber come over with a pump."

"Well, for heaven's sake!" his father cried in a voice that was choked with amused exasperation. "Why've you had me rattling these poor tired brains for nothing? Get the plumber and his damn pump over here!"

As Stephen went into the cottage, he debated whether

he should tell his father that he had already thought of the pump and called Mr. Spaulding earlier. In the end, he decided against it. For one thing, he did not want to detract from his father's jubilance, which pleased him; and for another, he was ashamed—considering the rationality of his father's diagnosis—to admit to the dark confusion and despair that had clouded his own thinking. Tangled in these considerations, he was startled when, having dialed the plumber's number, Mr. Spaulding's voice broke in on him from the other end of the line. He began to explain what had gone wrong with the siphon, but as he talked he found himself rambling through a complicated tale.

Finally Mr. Spaulding interrupted him. "You probably just got a big air bubble in there," he said. "Often happens around this time of year. Water level drops and there's not enough pressure left to expel the bubble."

"Yes," Stephen replied numbly. "That's what my father says." Bubble, he thought. Blood pressure. Blockage . . . In spite of himself, the words had a profoundly enervating effect.

"Tell you what," the plumber went on. "If you want to take a run over here, I'll lend you that old electric pump of mine. If an air bubble's what you've got, it should do the trick."

"Thanks very much," Stephen replied. "We'll be over in a little while." He hung up the phone and rejoined his father in the yard.

When Linda and Mrs. Bradford returned from their shopping trip, Stephen and his father drove to the plumber's house in his father's car. The distance was nearly fifteen miles round trip, and because Mr. Bradford drove slowly, they did not get back until dusk. By that time the baby had been fed supper and put to bed, and Linda had turned lights on in the cottage and lit the kerosene stove to ward off the evening chill. Stephen carried the pump from the car and set it on the ground beside the cottage. Then, following Mr. Spaulding's instructions, he connected the garden hose, screwed the open end into the suction valve of the pump, and primed the pump with a can of water. Afterward he ran an extension cord out through a window, plugged the pump into it, and switched on the current. There was a soft whirring sound as the pump motor started up, and then a succession of snorting noises as the pump began to suck air from the hose. After a few moments there were several tentative spurts of water, and then an interminable period in which the pump labored and the hose alternately gasped air and spouted water. During this time Stephen watched the pump almost breathlessly, scarcely daring to look at his father, who stood beside him, calmly puffing on his pipe. Finally the spurts became more frequent, and when they merged at last into a steady, continuous flow, Stephen switched off the pump, unhitched the hose, and plugged it into the faucet connection. Then, shouting triumphantly through the window, he told Linda that she could turn on the water.

Night fell swiftly as Stephen stood in the yard with his father. The water's running again, he thought happily, and for a second he was tempted to add a silent, sing-song corollary. Ah, but was all right with the world?

Suddenly Stephen found himself trembling in the damp nocturnal chill that rose from the ground. No, nothing was simple or certain, and he knew that he must never again reduce his hope and despair for life to abstractions that masked fear and wishful thinking. Nothing was certain. Life could easily be forfeit to the next moment and, if dry weather continued, another bubble of air might insinuate itself into the siphon. There was no continuity, Stephen decided, other than the continuity of time and whatever it might bring. What mattered, then—what he must always remember—were such moments as this one in which he and his father looked through a window that was growing opaque with condensation, and saw the soft shadows of their women setting table. For now the baby slept peacefully in the tiny back bedroom, and all of them were suspended together, as if in a cradle, on this balcony in the forest beneath the cruel and limitless sky. The two men continued to stand in the yard until the window had frosted over; then Stephen touched his father's arm, and they went inside.

The Sick Fox If it had not been for the
sun, Harry Barradine would not have seen the fox to
begin with, but the sun was still high above the mountain at the western end of the valley, and the buds on
saplings and bushes were not yet large enough to plunge
the stream into the leaf-covered twilight of summer. The
stream entered the valley from the Pfalzer hill country,
to the west, flowed past the American military post where
Barradine had his office, and fed into a larger stream in
the flat land near the Rhine. The fox lay by the water's
edge at the bottom of the bank, and at first Barradine
thought it was a garment someone had thrown away.
Then he saw it move. (He did not really see it move, he
saw it breathing.) The fox was rust-colored in the sun
and lay curled into a ball, so when Barradine squinted
down through the bushes lining the bank, he saw a pair
of pointed ears sticking from its loins. He laid his fly rod
in the grass of the meadow bordering the bank, and

moved closer for a better look. It's a fox, all right, he thought, but it's a careless fox to get caught sleeping in a place like that.

Barradine picked up a stick and threw it over the edge of the bank, toward the fox. The animal did not stir. It's deaf, Barradine thought, or the stream is making too much noise on the gravel. He threw a larger stick, and this time the fox jerked its head from its loins and looked into the water.

"Hey!" Barradine said.

The fox twisted its head toward the man standing above it.

"Hey!" Barradine said.

The fox got to its feet and, without looking at the man again, crept upstream and hid behind a stump. Barradine could see the tip of its tail through the bushes. This fox is an ostrich, he thought, or a remarkably intelligent fox who knows that I'm not carrying a gun and that if I start down the bank he has only a couple of yards to jump to reach the other side. "You're a damned insolent fox," Barradine said, aloud, and went off to find a branch.

When he returned, Barradine was carrying a length of sapling. He knelt in the grass at the top of the bank, pushed the branch down through the bushes, and drove it against the stump. The fox left its cover and loped along the edge of the water, watching the man, who was running now along the top of the bank.

"Hey!" shouted Barradine again.

The fox crouched, jumped, and landed with a splash in midstream; then it scrambled to the farther bank, paused to shake itself, and climbed slowly through the bushes to the meadow on the other side.

He's sick, Barradine thought. No fox in his right mind lets himself get wet.

The fox was moving downstream, and Barradine followed, paralleling it until the brook cut through a thicket of scrub. At this point the animal lowered itself in a patch of sunlight by a large hole and regarded the man on the other side.

"Old sport," said Barradine, "that's a face full of wisdom you've got. I hope you dry off and get better."

Ahead of him now Barradine could see part of the military post, a former German *Kaserne,* which lay at the eastern end of the valley. He could see the white flagpole, and the slate roofs of the cement barracks, where the soldiers were writing Sunday letters and listening to radio music beamed from the Armed Forces Network stations in Frankfurt, Stuttgart, and Berlin. In the second story of the Headquarters Building, the windows of his office were shining yellow in the sun of late afternoon. For a moment Barradine pictured the telephone sitting on his desk and wondered, as he often did when not in the office, if his chief, the Agent in Charge of Area Counter Intelligence, was trying to reach him. Putting business from his mind, he turned and retraced his steps to the place where he had left his fly rod; then he continued upstream, keeping an eye on the brook and knowing he would hear the *Kaserne* bugler calling the soldiers to the mess at evening.

Half an hour later Barradine was crouching against the bank at the head of a pool and watching his line sweep downstream with the current. When the line reached the tail of the pool, he drew up on the rod tip, felt a trout, and lifted it quickly to the bank. It was a brown trout, colored dark, like the shale at the bottom of the brook. Barradine cut a forked stick from an alder, threaded it through the gills, and laid the trout on the grass. He lit a cigarette and sat with his back against the bank, watching the pool. At the western end of the valley, the mountain was blue in the evening, and Sunday strollers were singing as they returned from the *Gasthaus* at the summit to the town below. Barradine baited his line, flicked it into the pool, and caught another trout. Then he heard sheep.

The sheep were moving down the opposite side of the valley in a solid wall stretching across the meadow from the stream to the woods. A pair of mongrel dogs paced up and down the edge of the woods, nipping at their flanks to keep them from the trees. Behind the flock a shepherd walked slowly along the bank. The shepherd was a sun-browned old man who wore a green cape and felt hat; a pair of binoculars was slung around his neck, and in the crook of his arm he carried a lamb. When he saw Barradine on the opposite bank, he stopped. The sheep moved on down the valley, and the two mongrels came running across the meadow to his side.

"Wie viele Fische haben Sie?" shouted the old man.

"Ich habe zwei," Barradine answered, holding up two fingers of his right hand.

The shepherd laid the lamb on its side in the meadow and moved closer to the bank, squinting in Barradine's direction. "You're an American!" he shouted, and

started down the bank. The mongrels preceded him across the stream, milled around Barradine's legs, and sniffed at the trout. The old man jumped across the shallows at the head of the pool and labored up the incline.
"I speak English!" he said.

"You speak good English," Barradine replied. All Germans speak English, he thought.

"I speak English," the shepherd shouted, "but in one ear am I deaf!"

"You speak good English!" Barradine shouted back.

"Listen!" said the old man. "One, two, three, four, five, six, seven, eight, nine, ten!"

Barradine grinned.

"Listen! Ten, twenty, thirty, forty, fifty . . . sixty, seventy, eighty, ninety, one hundred!"

"Very good," Barradine said.

"One thousand!" shouted the old man. "Ten thousand! One hundred thousand! *One million!*"

"*Eins, zwei, drei, vier, fünf—*" Barradine began.

"Listen!" the shepherd shouted. "I can count French!" He began to count, throwing a finger toward Barradine's chest with each number, and when he had finished he grinned happily and closed his eyes as if tired from a great effort. When he opened them, he looked at Barradine and grinned again. The eyes were blue and set deep in his head, and were triangular, like gabled windows.

"Where did you learn English?" Barradine asked.

"From a long time," said the old man. "At the end of the war I am the only one in Grumbach who can speak it. Every morning and every night I went to the Americans and translated for them their difficulties."

"Grumbach is a long way from here."

"I follow my sheep. They lead me everywhere."

Barradine looked at the binoculars slung around the old man's neck. I wonder why the shepherd carries binoculars, he thought. "You have a fine-looking pair of glasses," he said.

"The ears grow old first and then the eyes," replied the shepherd. "If it were not for the glasses, I would certainly lose some lambs in the trees and bushes."

"Are they Zeiss?" Barradine asked.

"No, not Zeiss. But they are German." The old man pulled the strap over his head and handed the binoculars to Barradine. "After the war they were valuable!" he shouted. "All the Americans wanted them!"

Barradine studied the binoculars and noted the mark of the German manufacturer stamped on the crosspiece. Why is it, he thought, you can never completely forget business—even out here? "They are fine glasses," he said, returning them.

"Until my eyes grew weak they were not a necessity," the old man replied. He looked at the trout lying on the grass. "How do you catch them?"

"With worms," Barradine answered.

The old man shook his head. "The trout are under the rocks." He made a scooping motion with his hands. "You must reach under the rocks and take them with your hands."

"The proprietor of the stream won't allow it," Barradine said, grinning.

"With your hands!" said the old man.

"It's *verboten!*" Barradine shouted.

The old man laughed. "Who owns this stream?"

"Herr Saul of Weiersheim."

"I don't know him. How much have you to pay?"

"Twenty marks for the season."

"It's too much. Take them with your hands!" The shepherd laughed and watched Barradine toss his cigarette butt into the water. "After the war I smoked a lot of them!" he shouted. "The Americans gave them to everybody! Five years ago I stopped smoking. Now I feel better. The ears and the eyes have grown old, but I have never been stronger in my life!" The old man held his elbows out from his sides when he said this, and started down the bank with his mongrels.

Barradine saw the lamb stir in the meadow on the other side of the stream. "There's a sick fox nearby," he said.

The shepherd jumped the brook and turned around. *"Ein Fuchs?"*

Barradine pointed downstream. "About three hundred meters."

"The dogs will have him," said the old man.

"He might have rabies."

"Rabies?"

"A sickness. It could be dangerous if he bit one of your lambs."

"Rabies . . ." the old man said.

"I will speak about it to the proprietor," said Barradine.

The shepherd looked as if he were about to jump back across the stream. "But you don't need to do that," he shouted, "for I myself will look at this fox, and when he don't get well I will kill him!"

"If he is sick with rabies, he will be dangerous," Barradine replied.

"Don't worry. When he don't get well, I will kill him!" The old man picked up the lamb, waved, and set off down the valley after his flock.

At evening Barradine followed the brook downstream toward the logging road where he had left his jeep. Tendrils of mist were curling over the edges of the meadow, and the woods were dark on either side and filled with the dankness of spring rain. When he came in sight of the *Kaserne,* he looked for the fox, and found it curled beside the hole. The fox had buried its nose beneath its tail, and the fur along the ridge of its back was being ruffled by a wind that crept through the valley. The shepherd has forgotten, Barradine thought. I'll stop at Saul's on my way home.

When Barradine reached the jeep, he dismantled his rod and laid it and the trout on the floorboards; then he drove out of the forest and past a football field on the hill above Weiersheim. Beyond the field there was a plateau of freshly manured land, and beyond that the road descended the hill to the cobblestoned streets of the village. He left the jeep in the market square and, carrying the two trout he had caught, walked to the end of an adjacent alley, where he found Herr Saul repairing his motorcycle in the yard before his cottage.

"Guten Abend, Herr Saul."

"Guten Abend, Herr Barradine!" Saul leaned the

motorcycle against the wall of his cottage and advanced, extending his hand. He was a short, stocky man who worked in the County Administration Offices, and he wore thick glasses that magnified his eyes out of all proportion. As if to mitigate the effect of oversized scrutiny, he always smiled, and now, as he saw the trout, he bent forward and smiled broadly. *"Petri Heil!"* he said, pronouncing the invocation to the patron saint of fishing.

"Petri Dank!" Barradine replied.

Saul fingered the larger trout. "It will weigh four hundred grams!" He spoke in German, and Barradine, speaking slowly and thinking out the words, answered him in German.

"I brought them as a gift," Barradine said.

"I thank you. They will make a fine breakfast." Saul took the trout and peered into Barradine's face, still smiling.

"Today I have seen a sick fox," Barradine said. "He is three hundred meters below the big pool."

"A fox," Saul repeated. "Yes, there are many of them in the woods."

"The one I saw is sick, perhaps with what we call rabies."

"Rabies? You will have to show me this word in the book." Saul led Barradine into the cottage and into a small living room, where he stooped to search a shelf for his dictionary. When he found it, he switched on a light and handed the book to Barradine, who leafed through the pages.

"Tollwut," Barradine said. *"Der Fuchs hat Tollwut, glaub' ich."*

"*Tollwut*," Saul echoed, peering at the dictionary. "Rabies . . . Yes," he said, in English. "That's very dangerous."

"Of course, I'm not sure of this. It is only possible the fox has *Tollwut*."

"Rabies," Saul repeated. "One moment, please, and I will write this word." He took a notebook from the shelf and looked again at the dictionary.

When Barradine glanced at the notebook, he saw rows of English words with their German meanings listed in neat columns beside them. "So you're studying English," he said.

Saul looked up from the notebook with an embarrassed smile. "Each word I write I will remember," he replied, tapping his head.

Barradine nodded, and went on, in German, "I met a shepherd at the stream who told me he would kill the fox if it didn't get well."

"Was the shepherd an old man?"

"An old man with two dogs."

"I believe he is a poacher, that one. If the fox has *Tollwut*, it cannot be left to him to kill it. The situation would be serious if this fox should bite a child."

"I didn't think of that," Barradine replied. "I told the shepherd because of his sheep."

"Very serious, this *Tollwut*. Since the land belongs to the town, I shall report it to the Town Secretary tomorrow, but it is also a matter for the authorities of the county. The *Kreisjäger* has jurisdiction for the wild animals. Yes, I must report it myself to both the Secretary and the Jäger in the morning." Saul drew himself up and

accompanied Barradine to the door. "Perhaps the
Kreisveterinär should also be informed," he said. "I
thank you for bringing this to my attention, Herr Barradine. *Auf Wiedersehen!*"

"*Auf Wiedersehen,*" said Barradine.

In the morning Barradine picked up his mail and messages at the Battalion Classified Message Center, on the
ground floor of the *Kaserne* Headquarters Building. The
corporal behind the desk always called him Mr. Barradine, but although Barradine wore civilian clothes and
worked alone, he was not a civilian. He was, in reality, a
military officer who had been given civilian status for
the performance of his mission. This fact, however, was
known only to his superiors at Counter Intelligence Headquarters; to the military personnel of the artillery battalion quartered in the *Kaserne* where he lived and had
his office, and to German officials of the towns and the
Kreis that made up his district, he was simply the Resident Intelligence Agent.

Upstairs, in his office, he read the mail and the morning newspaper, and started leafing through the messages;
there were the usual bulletins, some reports of May Day
demonstrations in the cities, and a letter of information
from Counter Intelligence Headquarters. At first glance
it seemed to be a typed form letter similar to the thousands of descriptions and summaries that filled the files.
Barradine scanned the letter and tossed it into the
basket on his desk. Then, frowning, he picked it up
again. At the top were two words of title: "Possible Sub-
versive." Beneath was a slender column of type describ-

99

ing "Subject"—a man named Pucher, whose first name and place of birth were unknown, who had been born in 1886, who was a shepherd, and whose address was listed in capitals as "GRUMBACH." Barradine read the letter once more, reached for his telephone, and dialed his chief at Counter Intelligence Headquarters.

"Mason, this is Barradine speaking. I have a letter here on a shepherd. You know anything about it?"

"What's the file number?"

Barradine read off a series of digits from the top right-hand corner of the letter. There was a short pause, during which he could hear the clacking of typewriters, and then Mason spoke again. "It's by way of an office memo Coolidge sent in last week."

"What's the alleged activity?"

"It seems the shepherd's been seen near a few of the *Kasernes.* Coolidge heard a rumble he might be political, but there's nothing definite."

"That's not much to go on," Barradine said. "Is he supposed to be political because he's been seen near some *Kasernes?*"

Mason laughed. "Coolidge turned it in as a matter of routine. He picked up the rumble in a *Gasthaus* and thought he'd pass it on just in case. Yours is the next district, so I forwarded you an information summary, in the event the shepherd shows up."

"He's here," Barradine said. "I saw him yesterday in a meadow. Nothing there but grass and sheep."

There was another laugh at the end of the line. "It's routine, Harry. It's a precaution. Frankly, I don't think it'll amount to anything, but we have to check it out."

"Look, Mason, I talked with the old guy. He follows a flock of sheep around the countryside. The sheep eat grass, and grass grows in the valleys, which is where you find the towns and where the Germans built the *Kasernes* —it's as simple as that. Besides, the shepherd couldn't leave his animals unattended ten minutes, let alone—"

"Harry, you've been in the business too long to forget we go by the book." Mason's voice was friendly but cool.

"I know," said Barradine. "And the book says you double-check everything and everybody. What'll I do— interrogate the old guy?"

Mason chuckled. "Stop giving me a hard time on Monday morning, Harry. You know damn well we haven't the right to interrogate civilians on our own these days. Now, look, I know you're busy, so don't go to a lot of trouble. Follow it up with the local police when you get the chance. I'll put through a records check and have Coolidge pin down the rumor at his end. If we get a cross-fix and the shepherd comes out clean, we can strike him off the casebook. But since Coolidge put him on paper to begin with, we'll have to get the machinery in motion and check him out."

Barradine hung up the phone and glanced again at the letter. You're getting careless, he thought. The book is always right—that's been proved before—and you know from experience the business can crop up anywhere and anytime. The trouble with you is you wanted that fishing stream to be some kind of sanctuary. . . . Barradine remembered the binoculars slung around the old man's neck, and felt annoyed with himself for remembering them.

At coffee call Barradine sat with the *Kaserne* doctor, a pale, red-eyed captain who had been drafted eighteen months previously, upon completion of medical school, and who had recently made his captaincy but had not yet forgiven the Department of the Army for delaying his career. "Here's one for you," the captain said. "I met a girl in Mannheim over the weekend. She asked me where I was stationed, and when I told her, you know what she said? She said I was 'behind the moon'!"

"*Hinter dem Mond.*" Barradine grinned. "That's how city Germans describe the farm districts."

"Which is poetic for boondocks behind the sticks! By the way, Barradine, what do you do for kicks out here in the boondocks?"

"I go fishing," Barradine replied.

"Well," said the captain, "not being a fisherman, I've put in a request for transfer. If it gets by the major at Area Command, I should be able to leave and go into one of the hospitals."

"Who'll stay up here to save lives?"

"You mean who'll stay up here twenty-four hours a day to tell dependent wives there's no known cure for the common cold!"

"You're a great reassurance to them," Barradine said, smiling. "In the event of plague, you'll be a hero."

The captain pushed his cup and saucer impatiently to one side. "There hasn't been anything more than a strep throat since I came here."

"Wait until the dependent kids get mumps."

"It's a diagnosis my replacement will make blindfolded."

"How about rabies?"

"Altogether different," said the captain. "That's a disease transmitted by dogs. They used to call it hydrophobia. You seen a sick dog or something?"

"I saw a sick fox in the valley yesterday."

"A sick fox, hanh?" The captain leaned forward and dropped his voice. "I guess you know a rabid animal of any sort can be sheer poison!"

Barradine noted the confidential lowering of the captain's voice. Like everyone else up here, the captain is bored, he thought. He's going to start impressing me with his medical knowledge.

"How far away was this fox?" the captain asked.

"A mile or so," Barradine said.

"What made you think he was sick? You notice any particular symptoms?"

Barradine laughed. "He wasn't foaming around the mouth, if that's what you mean, but he didn't run away. He acted as if he were fed up with everything."

The captain continued in his serious vein. "If he should infect one of the dogs around here, we'd be in a bad way. There's a vaccine for rabies, but it should be administered quickly. With this fox on the loose . . ."

"I don't know if the fox has rabies or not," Barradine said. "All I know is he's sick."

After lunch Barradine drove up the hill to the Gendarmerie Station on the outskirts of Weiersheim. When he entered the dark hallway, he rapped on the door marked "POLIZEIAMT" and walked inside; Polizeiwachtmeister Bauer, who was sitting at his desk talking

into the telephone, looked up and pointed to a chair.
Barradine sat, lit a cigarette, and gazed at the wall before him, which was covered with carefully wrought
diagrams of traffic accidents showing the precise position of vehicles at the point of impact, the direction in
which they were originally traveling, the distance and
direction traveled after impact, and the exact position of
the slightly injured, the disabled, and the dead. Then his
glance fell, as it always did, upon the wall above the heat-
ing stove, where there was a photograph showing Bauer
in his Wehrmacht tunic and officer's peaked hat. Barradine looked at the desk where Bauer's automatic pistol
lay hidden in its shining black holster and, finally, at
Bauer himself, who, in his policeman's green uniform,
sat leaning over the desk and barking into the telephone.
Except for what Barradine knew to be a difference in
color, the uniform was nearly identical with the one in
the photograph. Barradine examined Bauer's long black
boots, shuffling in irritation on the floor beneath the desk,
and the tiny, well-oiled folds where the leather creased
above the ankles. Then Bauer hung the receiver on a
wall hook and turned the crank handle to cut off the call.
The two men stood and shook hands.

"So, Herr Barradine . . ."

"I stopped in a moment to ask you about a shepherd
whom I have seen in the valley," Barradine said. With the
Wachtmeister he always spoke German.

"In the Weiersheim valley?"

"An old man who comes from Grumbach."

"Ah, that one! That one comes twice a year. He comes
once in the spring and once again in late summer after
the hay is cut."

"What do you know of him?"

The *Wachtmeister* shrugged, smiling. "At night the shepherd leaves his sheep in Leuthner's barn and goes to drink beer at the Gasthof Post."

Barradine took a package of cigarettes from his shirt pocket and proffered the open end to Bauer, who selected a cigarette and held it carefully between his lips as he applied the match flame. All right, use the direct approach, Barradine thought. This Bauer is not a diplomat from Bonn. "Does the shepherd have a criminal record?" he asked.

"The shepherd has no criminal record here," replied Bauer, "but who knows what record he may have elsewhere? You would have to visit every village in the Pfalz! One time some farmers claimed he had not obtained the proper grazing permits, and another time the *Kreisjäger* suspected him of snaring rabbits—but nothing was proved." The policeman shrugged. "Who can tell about shepherds? They are always moving from one place to another."

"What do you know of his politics?"

"Ah!" Bauer smiled. "His politics . . . Who knows about the politics of shepherds? They are always alone. This one sometimes goes to the *Gasthaus*, but I have never heard of his discussing politics. Who knows about the politics of a shepherd? His dogs, the sheep perhaps . . ." Bauer laughed through the smoke of the cigarette.

The *Wachtmeister* is having a fine time, Barradine thought, and it is your own damn fault. Coolidge is a fool for having written up a report on the basis of hearsay, and you are a fool for coming here with these stupid questions. I'll be damned if you're going to give Police

105

Sergeant Bauer the pleasure of telling you why it is the shepherd carries binoculars.

"Does the shepherd have any physical defects?" Barradine asked.

"Defects?" Bauer repeated, shrugging. "His ears, perhaps. In the *Gasthaus* they shout at him to make themselves understood."

"And the eyes?"

"*Ja,* also the eyes! Once, during the rabbit business, I demanded his papers and found an administrative mistake on his identity card. When I brought this to the shepherd's attention, he had difficulty in seeing it." Bauer was smiling again. "You have some suspicion, *nicht?*"

This time it was Barradine who shrugged. "Nothing important," he said. "A few rumors." The shepherd was telling the truth, he thought.

"You know the shepherd's name?" asked Bauer.

"Pucher."

"*Ja,* I remember it now. Perhaps he has come over from the East. As I say, there is no telling about these shepherds. When there are no barns, they sleep in the woods."

"It is undoubtedly a rumor," Barradine said. "Do you expect any local disturbances to follow those that took place in the cities on May Day?"

Bauer was at the window, looking into the street. "These shepherds are like animals," he muttered. "They are never of any one town or place, so it is entirely possible the rumors are correct. I will make some inquiries. Perhaps I will find the shepherd has failed to obtain the

proper grazing rights." He turned and smiled at Barradine, who had risen.

"I'm sure it's a rumor," Barradine said. You can't
beat this Bauer's thought processes, he told himself.
Now that the bastard thinks you know something he
doesn't know, he's willing to nail the shepherd with anything he can lay his hands on. "Please let me know if
any political demonstrations are scheduled," he said.

"I will telephone you, Herr Barradine, and I will mention our shepherd to the authorities. One must keep a constant eye on such wanderers."

The *Wachtmeister* came outside and stood on the stoop
as Barradine went down to the street. When Barradine
turned to say goodbye, he saw the black boots on a level
with his eyes, at the top of the steps. Polizeiwachtmeister
Bauer was smiling down at him from the same height as
that from which Barradine had first looked down at the
fox. The boots were immaculate in the sunlight.

When Barradine returned to the *Kaserne,* he found a
note tacked to his door requesting his presence in the
office of the battalion colonel. The colonel was a conscien-
tious officer who took considerable pride in knowing
every facet and characteristic of his *Kaserne* and command; hence he rarely summoned the Resident Intelligence Agent except when something turned up in the
latter's field that made this knowledge appear incomplete.
During such interviews Barradine always revolved in
ever diminishing circles around the subject, leaving innumerable loopholes to afford the colonel an opportunity
of claiming prior knowledge at some convenient point. It

was an old military game, in which each participant was
fully aware of the other's intention, and it was played
without rancor.

Barradine went to the colonel's office and waited outside until the adjutant asked him to step in. The colonel,
a small, severe man, sat dwarfed behind an immense ma-
hogany desk with two 75-millimeter-shell bookends before him and a pair of crossed flags at his back. He
pressed his lips together as Barradine came over the
carpet, and Barradine recognized the pressing of the lips
as an unfavorable sign.

"You wanted to see me, sir?"

"Yes, Barradine," said the colonel. "I received a telephone call this afternoon from the commander of the
Area Medical Attachment. He's sending an inspection
team out here at zero-eight-hundred hours tomorrow
morning. It seems our good doctor phoned in some
damned nonsense about you seeing an animal with rabies."

Barradine smiled. "I told the doctor I'd seen a sick
fox."

"Well, the medics have made the usual flap out of it."
The colonel cast a humorless glance at Barradine and
rustled through some disposition forms lying on his desk.
"Group sent instructions by courier an hour ago. First of
all, I'm supposed to furnish someone who'll lead the inspection team to the fox. Then I have to corral all the dog
owners in my command and determine whether all dogs
are properly registered. And, finally"—the colonel said
this reproachfully, looking Barradine in the face—"I've
got to prepare a list showing dog owners, kind of dogs

owned, and date of last rabies injection."

"My God!" said Barradine. "I only mentioned it in passing!"

"So did the doctor," the colonel observed dryly. "It's how flaps get started. Since you're the one who indirectly got the ball rolling, I'd appreciate it if you'd be at the gate at zero-eight-hundred to meet the inspection team. I'll furnish some men, and you can lead the expedition out to wherever it is you saw this animal while I have the list made up." The ghost of a smile appeared on the colonel's face.

"I'm sorry about the trouble, sir, and I'll do what I can to help," Barradine said. "I want to assure you, however, that my official functions have nothing to do with diseased foxes."

"I know that," the colonel replied. "Mine have nothing to do with canine injections. I'm not a veterinarian. I'm trying to ready this post for the inspector general's party next week."

Upstairs, as Barradine unlocked the door to his office, he heard his telephone ring. He went in, moved quickly across the room, and picked up the receiver.

"*Ja, Herr Barradine,*" a voice said. "Here is Saul. I have been trying to reach you this afternoon, for I have important news of the fox."

Barradine swung the phone cord around the corner of his desk and sat heavily in his swivel chair.

"I have spoken with the Town Secretary and the Jäger, Herr Barradine. Our Secretary is much interested and has written a proclamation ordering the children from the *Wald* until the matter is settled. He has asked me to tell

you that he would be pleased for you to meet the Jäger
and Wachtmeister Bauer tomorrow morning. They would
like to see this fox and shoot it. The Town Secretary also
believes the *Kommandant* of the *Kaserne* should be noti-
fied, but as I do not have his telephone number, I thought
perhaps . . ."

"The *Kommandant* already knows of the fox," Barradine replied. "At what time does the Jäger wish me to
meet him?"

"At your convenience, Herr Barradine."

"Tell him I'll be in the square shortly after eight
o'clock," Barradine said, and hung up the phone.

The sun was falling behind a barracks building, and a
final ray of light slanted through the window, striking
Barradine on the small of the back. For some minutes
after he hung up the phone, he sat in his swivel chair and
thought of the fox recuperating in the warm afternoon.

The morning was cool and hazy, as spring mornings are
in the Rhineland, where night slips off the open fields
leaving a wake of mist. Barradine sat in his jeep at the
front gate of the *Kaserne*, watching two white-helmeted
M.P.s check the passes of incoming personnel and wave
on outgoing cars filled with dependent wives bound for
the shopping centers at Mannheim and Heidelberg.
Across the roadway some manure wagons were passing
out to the fields, the men sitting in the wagons and holding the reins of oxen, the women wearing kerchiefs and
plodding in the road behind, and the cargoes steaming in
the morning chill. Presently a jeep turned off the highway
and started down the hill toward the *Kaserne*. When

Barradine made out the white circle and red cross em-
blazoned on the canvas top, he stepped into the road and
signaled the vehicle to a halt; a lieutenant in field uniform and sunglasses opened the door.

"Good morning," Barradine said. "Are you the veterinarian?"

"I'm a physician," the lieutenant replied unhappily.
"The vet is checking cows today."

Barradine looked at the unhappy lieutenant and suppressed a smile. Then he turned and waved toward the
parking lot inside the gate, where a sergeant and two
soldiers—the men the colonel had promised him—were
waiting by a three-quarter-ton truck. "All right," he said
to the lieutenant. "Tell your driver to follow me and we'll
get this over with as quickly as possible."

When the three military vehicles ground to a halt on
the cobblestones of the square in Weiersheim, Barradine
saw the Jäger and Polizeiwachtmeister Bauer sitting side
by side on motorcycles. As Barradine got out of his jeep,
the two men kicked the stands beneath their cycles and
dismounted. The Jäger wore brown leather breeches and
the green jacket and hat of his profession and carried a
shotgun slung over his back. A large, confident Airedale
sat patiently in a carrier attached to his motorcycle.
Barradine glanced at the two pairs of immaculate boots
and shook hands with both the Jäger and Wachtmeister
Bauer.

"We must wait for the Town Secretary," Bauer said,
grinning and rubbing his hands briskly in the morning
chill. "Our Secretary has undoubtedly prepared a speech
for the occasion."

111

As the policeman spoke, Barradine saw the Secretary and Saul emerge from a building across the square. Saul was also wearing boots—not the high, tight-fitting boots of the policeman or the Jäger but the heavy kind worn by peasants in the fields. Bauer grinned again and repeated his joke about the Secretary's speech, but Barradine pretended not to understand. Behind him he heard the door of the truck slam shut, and turned to see the sergeant and the soldiers lean their carbines against a fender and light cigarettes.

"*Guten Morgen, Herr Barradine*," said Saul, out of breath from walking across the cobblestones.

"*Guten Morgen*," Barradine replied, and shook hands with Saul and the Secretary.

"And why do the soldiers carry weapons?" the Jäger demanded. His lean face had flushed, and he directed the question not to Barradine but to the Town Secretary. The Secretary, who had been on the verge of speaking, minimized the soldiers with an impatient wave of his hand, and smiled.

"No doubt because the *Kommandant* has ordered them to do so," Barradine said, to Saul.

The Jäger's gray eyes narrowed. He turned again to the Secretary. "It is not necessary that the soldiers carry weapons. I myself will dispose of the fox—if, indeed, there is any fox to be disposed of."

A point well made, Barradine thought. If there is no fox to be disposed of, the game warden is not going to be disappointed. That's a military face, the warden's; it's the face of a man who has counted tanks in his day and who now counts hares and roebuck and who isn't any happier about your finding a sick fox in his territory than the colonel was when you . . . "It is customary for soldiers to carry weapons, is it not?" Barradine said, addressing Saul again.

"Yes, certainly," Bauer said. "But the Herr Jäger must do the killing. This is also customary, Herr Barradine."

"Naturally," Barradine replied.

"You may be interested to know that we have found something about the shepherd," Bauer went on, his voice faintly placating. "Our shepherd has indeed failed to obtain the proper permissions this season, so we shall have the opportunity now to question him."

"I am no longer interested in the shepherd," Barradine said. "It appears to me the rumors against him have no foundation."

"I will require the soldiers to leave their weapons in the truck," the Jäger announced, and then said something that Barradine did not understand.

"The soldiers are under the orders of the *Kaserne Kommandant*," Barradine replied. "Let's get going." He climbed into his jeep, opened the door for Saul, and started the engine.

"*Gute Jagd!*" the Town Secretary shouted.

Barradine waved to the Secretary, wheeled the jeep around, and started up the hill out of town. Yes, it'll be a good hunt, he thought. It's going to be one hell of a pleasant safari. At this point the clients would like to substitute the White Hunter for the fox. The doctor is offended because you mistook him for a veterinarian; the Jäger was offended when the fox was reported in the first place, and now his professional pride is outraged because the soldiers have brought along their weapons; to top it off, the *Wachtmeister* appears honor bound to prove something derogatory against the shepherd. The fox may be a loser, too, but by this time he's probably taking his rest cure in another *Kreis*. It's your own damn fault for not having left him alone to begin with. . . .

Saul and Barradine arrived first at the meadow and waited for the others. It was cold and quiet in the valley, and steam was rising from the hollow of the brook. The motorcycles of the Jäger and the *Wachtmeister* appeared at the edge of the forest and slithered across the wet grass, leaving serpentine trails in the dew. When the party had assembled, Barradine walked to the truck and told the sergeant to keep his men in the background and to allow the Jäger to do the shooting if there was any shooting to be done. Then he started upstream, followed by the Jäger and the dog, who was sniffing eagerly at the bushes, and the others strung out behind like a column on patrol.

When he drew opposite the point where he had last seen the fox, he descended the bank and jumped the brook. The others came after him, except for the sergeant and the soldiers, who remained on the bank smoking cigarettes. For several minutes Barradine searched through the scrub; then he stopped and, in puzzlement, pointed to the place where the hole had been but where there was now a mound of red earth and a cleared area showing the scars of fresh digging. Turning, he noted the serious face of the lieutenant from the medical detachment, the disappointed face of Saul, and the disdainful faces of the Jäger and Bauer. Whining, the Jäger's dog began to paw the ground at his feet.

Upon a quiet command from its master, the dog went to the edge of the meadow and lay down, watching the assemblage that had gathered in a semicircle around the clearing. The Jäger took up a stick from the brush and prodded the pile of dirt; then he removed the shotgun from his shoulder, stood it against a tree, and, with both hands on the stick, began to scoop the earth backward between his legs. Below the surface he uncovered traces of fur and, after more digging, unearthed the fox sprawled forlornly in a shallow grave, with mud caking its wet and matted pelt.

"But you were right, it is certainly a fox!" said Saul, clapping Barradine on the back as if to reaffirm a confidence that had begun to waver.

"The shepherd has done as he promised," Barradine replied.

"Our instructions are to take the animal to the *Kreisveterinär* for examination," said Bauer, glancing at the lieutenant from the medical detachment. "Naturally, Herr Barradine, the results of this examination will be made known to the American authorities."

The Jäger had taken a length of leather thong from his pocket and passed it carefully beneath the corpse. Now he drew it about the forelegs and knotted it tightly. Then, leading the way, he descended to the stream, swung the fox to the farther side, and jumped across. The soldiers cast indifferent glances at the dead animal as he dragged it through the bush. Bauer hurried to his side. "Our shepherd has killed and buried the fox, Herr Jäger, but perhaps his mongrels have engaged the animal! Perhaps

115

it has bitten one of the sheep!"

The Jäger deposited his burden beside the motorcycles and nodded. Bauer began to speak in a torrent of German which Barradine could not understand.

"What the *Wachtmeister* thinks may be true," said Saul. "If some of the animals of the shepherd have come in contact with the fox, they may indeed be infected. We are back where we began, Herr Barradine!"

"Who knows if the fox had rabies or not?" Barradine replied. "How will anyone know until the veterinarian has examined the animal and given his report?"

"But, Herr Barradine, that the fox had rabies was your opinion in the beginning!"

"So it was," said Barradine wearily.

The Jäger and Bauer were conversing with slurred German vehemence when the latter suddenly stepped aside and pointed up the valley. The sun, mounting in the east, had cast a long corridor of light toward the mountain, and far away, where the meadow diminished into the woods, Barradine saw the shepherd and his flock outlined like a minuscule crèche against the grass. Saul rushed to Bauer's side and squinted along his outstretched arm.

"Our shepherd has not moved on fast enough this time!" Bauer shouted. He smiled at Barradine.

"Wait!" Barradine said. "When the fox was first discovered, the shepherd stated he would kill it if it did not become well. What justice can there be in troubling him now, when he has only carried out his promise and thereby saved us trouble?"

"But, Herr Barradine, certain elements of the situation

116

remain to be determined, and the finding of the fox *dead* merely brings new complications to light. . . ." The voice of Polizeiwachtmeister Bauer was soothing, and the smile was still on his face. "To begin with, there is the matter of grazing permits that the shepherd has failed to obtain. Secondly, there is a question as to whether the animals of the old man have come in contact with the diseased fox. Then, there is serious doubt whether the shepherd had the right to dispose of the fox without consulting the proper authorities." Here Bauer looked significantly at the Jäger. "And, finally, Herr Barradine, is there not some doubt remaining as to your own suspicions? Would it not benefit you professionally to interrogate the shepherd at this time?"

"I am convinced that any professional suspicions concerning the shepherd have been unwarranted," replied Barradine. The *Wachtmeister* has a technical point, he thought. Should you pass up the chance to double-check?

Polizeiwachtmeister Bauer was smiling politely. "Naturally, you must do as you think best, Herr Barradine. I merely thought you might wish to observe, since we must apprehend the shepherd anyway—" Bauer broke off, shrugging. "It is a perfect opportunity, *nicht?*"

"For God's sake!" Barradine began, and then looked at the lean, determined face and gray eyes of the Jäger. You fool, he thought. The worst thing you could have done was give the Jäger the idea you wanted to protect the shepherd.

"Sixty miles to see a buried animal!" the lieutenant from the medical detachment complained bitterly.

"Go to hell!" said Barradine.

The lieutenant adjusted his sunglasses, jumped into his jeep, and ordered the driver to start away. Saul looked at Barradine and hesitated as the Jäger and Polizeiwachtmeister Bauer began walking over the meadow toward the mountain; then he turned and hurried after the two figures plowing steadily through the wet grass.

Barradine looked up the valley at the flock and saw a glint of light. He strained to make out the shepherd and saw another flash, which came from the midst of the sheep, as if the sun were reflecting against a shining object. The sharp light cut into him and made him wince. It's the binoculars, he thought miserably. The shepherd's seen the three of them and he can see you also. Why in the name of God and in the first place could you not have allowed the fox the privilege of diagnosing his own ailments and being sick in peace?

The three Germans were striding briskly over the meadow, their heavy boots cutting parallel trails in the covering of dew. For a moment Barradine watched the rapidly diminishing figures, and then he started slowly up the valley; following their straight, purposeful swath, he found himself shivering in the first warmth of day.

Behind the Moon The train is rocketing
through Champagne—that land of battlefield and eroded
scarp which, even in peacetime, looks worn and sad. During the night, while I was dozing, we stopped at Nancy
and lost some French soldiers who had got on at Baden-
Baden, wearing baggy uniforms and smoking those
wretched Gauloises that smell like rope. Now there is just
the girl and I, and I am halfway between sleep and wak-
ing, and the first metallic light of a September day is filling the compartment, which still holds the night chill and
the stale odor of the soldiers' interminable cigarettes.
There's a cancerous pallor to this *champenois* daybreak.
It's perfect. Just as I had always imagined it would be.
Ah, these grim towns of the north of France—I see them
briefly through a filthy window—crumbling stone houses
huddled together like blocks of pumice soaking up the
moisture and the color of the earth and sky.

I'm shifting uncomfortably now on the wooden bench,

and rubbing the sleep from my eyes. Then I look at the girl, who is eating breakfast—some little biscuits and some fruit which she carries in a *filet*. She has golden hair and a face without flat planes—all rounded, pink and lovely. She smiles—a shy, tentative smile. She offers me a piece of fruit across the aisle between us—a pear.

"*Danke schön*," I say. I know the girl is German because I heard her speak to the conductor when she got on the train with me at Stuttgart.

"*Bitte*," the girl replies. That's a nice word. It's the friendliest and least harsh word in the entire language, and the girl says it sing-song.

Thus encouraged, I try some sentences. The vocabulary is straight from a Berlitz Reader I have been studying in my spare time. The sentences are badly put. The verbs are not all strung together at the end as they should be. I am telling the girl what I feel about the country through which we are passing. This is, I'm afraid, quite a clue about me. Who save an American would try to tell a strange German girl about the sadness of Champagne?

"You are an American!" the girl says in perfect English, laughing brightly (I assume) at my misplaced verbs.

We converse the rest of the way to Paris. For the most part, it is an exchange of information. Her name is Ursula. She is going to Paris for the first time. She has been to college at Plymouth, England. She loves to travel and she has been to Spain. Next summer she will go to Italy. Since 1959 she has been a librarian at the American Dependent School in Bad Cannstatt, which is only a few kilometers from Ludwigsburg, where I am stationed. Her mother lives in the American sector of Berlin. Her father

and brother were killed in the war. Berlin is, like Champagne, a sad place, but there are many sad places in Europe, and one must not become too serious about them.
She herself is never serious because there is no pleasure
in it. . . .

The train pulls into the Gare de l'Est. I carry Ursula's
bags along the platform and into the station hall, where
she is being met by friends. Then I wave goodbye and
leave. I am already planning to call on her at the library
when I return to Ludwigsburg. (The captain of my detachment, who sends one of us each week to the post exchange at Bad Cannstatt for supplies, will be surprised,
next time, when I am first to volunteer.) Now I have
reached the Boulevard de Strasbourg, and on the hill
sloping away from the station I see my first sidewalk café.
Paris. For the moment I have almost forgotten that Ursula exists—it will not be the last time.

The details of our next meeting are few. There am I in
freshly starched khaki, garrison cap in hand, tiptoeing
stiffly into the library of the American School at Bad
Cannstatt. And there is Ursula wearing a full-skirted
summer dress with a flower print in it. For the first time I
notice how ample she is. Now she smiles that lovely smile,
and we engage in whispered conversation about how
much each of us liked Paris. Finally we go outside into a
corridor, where I ask Ursula if she will have supper with
me Saturday night. The effect of my invitation is dis-
concerting. Ursula is blushing. Then she's laughing.
Never have I known a girl who laughs so easily. But yes,
she accepts. It would be lovely. At this moment the corridor erupts as the third, fourth, and fifth grades are let out

of classroom for lunch. I bid Ursula goodbye and allow myself to be swept outside with the children.

The first evening we spend together is a fine success, which leads to other evenings and now to a passage of time—four months, to be precise—the end of summer and the whole of fall, during which we see each other constantly. How shall I describe this autumnal interlude? For one thing, it is a catalogue of innocence, a wholesome romp through the pages of an illustrated travelogue. But I should offer a word or two of explanation here by admitting frankly that I am one of those people whom Europe has overwhelmed right from the start, from the moment I stepped off the troopship at Bremerhaven. And when I am stationed at Ludwigsburg—well, there is Duke Ludwig's palatial copy of Versailles surrounded by a web of tiny, cobblestoned streets that are lined with cottages with red tile roofs and filled with chickens, cattle, and children in *Lederhosen*. And not only in Ludwigsburg, but everywhere I go—Stuttgart, Champagne, Paris —the vision I have always held of Europe comes true. Into this scenic sepia Ursula slips like a slide into its projector slot. She's my gay companion, my girl guide to Germany, my giggling *Gänschen*. But I started to describe what I did with this girl as a catalogue of innocence, and God only knows why I feel I am stretching the limits of credulity here, or why, for that matter, we are always faintly ashamed of innocence. All right, then, on with it. It is surely conceivable that Ursula and I ate picnics amid flowers on the banks of the Neckar. Why not, hey? But listen, whole *acres* of flowers! Folding meadows of hay and flowers, fragrant and so many feet high that we have to stand to see the river below. And what do we do, hidden even from the birds, in this glorious expanse of sweet stalk? Why, she teaches me German.

Ich habe die Burg auf dem Berg gesehen

I have . . . the castle . . . on the mountain . . . seen—

a charmingly alliterative little sentence that stems from a trip we've made to the Hohenstaufen Castle in the Black Forest. From this point on, my German improves rapidly, because each weekend we're off on a new excursion. We attend the opera and, between acts of *Ondine,* watch swans floating on a pond in the *Theaterplatz.* We take a train to Freiburg, and then a bus to Breisach, where we examine altar carvings in an old church that sits upon a cliff above the Rhine. We visit the brick cathedral at Speyer, the *Schloss* at Heidelberg, and the university at Tübingen. Sunday nights, on the way home, we take a yellow trolley which climbs through dark, winding streets to the Stuttgart suburbs. When we get off the trolley, we walk up a steep hill to a large stucco house where Ursula lives. And then, late one evening, as we stand before her doorway, planning the next weekend's adventure, Ursula tells me she lives behind the moon.

That's the German way of saying "in the sticks."

Behind the moon . . . I walk back down to the car tracks in a cloud. That phrase has a purple-funk effect on me—I who have no immunity to charm—which lasts until I reach the *Hauptbahnhof,* where my comrades in arms and their girl friends are waiting for the late train to Ludwigsburg.

"Achtung! Achtung!"

123

(That's the stationmaster announcing departures and arrivals.)

"Achtung!"

It's a flat, deadly voice booming out beneath the stars, foretelling doom and, for a moment, hushing even the tipsy, tittering couples walking, arms entwined, along the concrete platform. Then the train comes and everyone climbs aboard and there is much singing during the trip to Ludwigsburg, where black Mercedes cabs line the curbs, waiting to whisk the "Amis" through fog-slicked streets to their barracks.

Behind the moon . . .

I go off to sleep thinking it over and over.

Behind the moon . . .

Why, out of this world.

My friends at the detachment office are a fine bunch. Bored to death with the army, of course. We have coffee every hour. And innumerable cigarettes. They've seen me with Usch in the streets of Stuttgart. Out late last night? they ask, winking. Ah, those ribald winks of friends.

Christmas comes.

Ursula goes home to Berlin, and I get a package in the mail. It is full of goodies and tiny, intricately woven stars of straw she has spent hours making. I hang the stars on the wall above my bunk. My friends come into the room and eat up all the dates, figs, and candies, and since it is Christmas and everyone is lonely and vulnerable, they are full of envy that even winking cannot hide. So I sit on my bunk, watching proudly as sweet Usch's Christmas package makes the rounds, and blushing with the false modesty that basks in the ribald winks of friends.

124

But in my case it's really false, for, having accepted the silent and knowing certification of my confreres for favors infinitely greater than a box of goodies, how can I, of all people, deny the basic worthlessness of the credit tendered in a twinkle?

When Usch returns to Stuttgart after the holidays, we make plans to spend a weekend at Kleines Wasertal, a ski resort on the Austrian frontier. It's a lovely spot—she's been there before—and we'll stay at a student dormitory and climb snow-covered trails on the mountainside, saying *"Grüss Gott!"* to everyone we meet. But the very next day I receive orders stationing me permanently in the Rheinland-Pfalz, more than 150 miles away. There's only time for a brief telephone call to Usch, for, in true military fashion, I have to leave, bag and baggage, that same afternoon.

The Pfalz is really behind the moon. It's in the middle of nowhere, and my new post is in the dead center of that. There's plenty to see on the periphery, however, and each winter weekend I go off to some new place—the Cathedral at Trier, or the casino at Bad Dürkheim, or one of the castles on the Rhine near Bingen. Meanwhile Usch and I correspond regularly. I write long letters telling her the places I've seen; she writes back describing the new apartment she has taken in Bad Cannstatt and her plans to go to Italy in July, and asking when I will return to Stuttgart and if I can come to Berlin with her in October.

As it happens, I do not return to Stuttgart until June, and then I am merely passing through to pick up leave orders that will allow me to go to Spain.

I have written Usch, of course, and we have made plans

to meet and attend a concert at the Cannstatt Kursaal. It turns out to be a strange evening. For one thing, there's a sudden and torrential downpour. For another, Usch has made a mistake and we arrive at the Kursaal to find the concert ending. How unlike Usch, who, in planning all the trips and forays we've made together, has always been so accurate and punctual. Haven't I often told her she's my favorite travel agent? But missing the concert makes little difference, for, as ever, Usch and I are our gay selves. We sit on a bench beneath a chestnut tree, laughing at the music lovers—all elegantly dressed—who are scurrying for taxis and getting wet. Then Usch suggests we go to her place. Her roommate is away and we'll be able to chat quietly there. The building sits on a hill above the Neckar Valley and Ursula lives on the fourth floor in a tiny apartment filled with plants. We sit on a small sofa.

"How nice," says Ursula with a bright smile, "that you are going off to Spain."

"Yes," I reply, and tell her enthusiastically about the route I plan to take.

"I'm sure it will be a splendid trip," she says.

Do I detect a touch of melancholy in her voice? But, of course, I've been so preoccupied with Spain that I've almost forgotten she is going to Italy.

"Tell me about your trip, Usch," I say.

"It's rather unsure," she replies. "I was going to Naples, but my mother wants me now to come to Berlin in August instead of October." She pauses and looks at me. "Could you come to Berlin in August?"

I shake my head. I explain that I am using up my leave

time for the trip to Spain.

"I'm sorry, Usch."

"Well, we can perhaps arrange something later," she says with a shrug.

But her eyes have become moist, and she gets up quickly and disappears into the bedroom. When she returns, she is carrying a package wrapped in bright paper and tied with colored ribbon.

It is a gift for me.

I sit on a sofa unwrapping it in guilty silence. Inside, there is a book of photographs of Spain. I look at them, exclaiming. Then I look at Usch, whose eyes are still damp. I try to encourage her about Italy.

"You really should go, Usch. Imagine visiting Florence, Venice, and Rapallo!"

But it is I who should go. My head is full of Geneva, Nîmes, and Barcelona, and I am in no shape to interpret the meaning of those moist blue eyes. Besides, my leave begins at midnight. Tomorrow I am off for Switzerland at six. I make the usual explanation.

"I'll see you in Berlin, Usch," I say gaily. "If not October, some other time."

We kiss goodbye, and then I am gone. As I cross the parking lot, outside, I look up, and there is Usch framed in the window. She is waving, and I wave back.

Goodbye, Usch.

I can see her even after I have passed into the shadows beyond the lot.

Goodbye, Usch . . .

As it turns out, I'll not see you in Berlin, or anywhere else. I shall never see you again.

But the story doesn't end. There's continuity to come, a bit raggedly, perhaps, but who imagines that the recurrences of our little scenarios are evenly spaced? I'll turn up the projector to full speed now and skip some scenery —Switzerland, France, Spain, Majorca, and back to the Pfalz for an autumn, a winter . . . hold it at December a moment. It's Christmastime, and there's another package, from Berlin again, where Usch is spending the holidays with her mother. A smaller package this time, but with much the same contents as before, and two of the woven straw stars, which remain for a couple of weeks stuck in a corner of the blotter on my desk, until the cleaning Frau decides they are something to be thrown away. Back to high speed on the projector and a long blur now, for there's much ground and time to cover—a continent and more than two and a half years. My military service is finished and I'm back in the States, living and working in New York, and it is autumn again—October—more than four years after Ursula offered me, in the dim light of that desolate *champenois* daybreak, the unsymbolic pear for which no one should have jumped to any fabled conclusions. I have not forgotten Usch, of course, but I no longer think of her. Well, delicately put, perhaps, but spoken too soon, for here's a letter forwarded by my family—a letter postmarked Berlin/Steglitz and bearing the return address of Ursula Müller.

Naturally, I am delighted—I who have nothing but fond memories of my sojourn in Europe. And I am curious, too. Why should Ursula try to reach me after all this time? There are many possibilities, of course, but one is particularly appealing. Ursula, who loves to travel, is

coming to America. How wonderful it will be to meet her
ship, to find her bubbling with amazement at the skyline,
to take her around New York . . .

I tear the letter open and begin to read. The first para-
graph is filled with hopes that the address she remembers
is not obsolete, and that even if the cause for which she
must now contact me is not of a pleasant nature, there
might again be an opportunity to hear from me. She re-
calls our picnics, our trips, our evenings together. She re-
minds me of that last night, when we missed the concert
at the Cannstatt Kursaal. And then she says: ". . . How
wonderful was it, but how terribly long ago."

For a moment I stop reading. Ah, why such sadness,
Usch? Beneath your quaint vagaries of grammar, which
I still find charming, you fill me with a sense of dread. I
take up the letter again and go on quickly to the end with
the breathless concentration that is buttress against bad
news. And when I finish, my eyes are filled with tears.

To make it short, Usch has a two-and-a-half-year-old
daughter, Sigrid, and though she loves her dearly, the
child has given rise to a lot of trouble. The father, a Nea-
politan lawyer named Orlando D'Ampezza, has denied
before an Italian court not only his fatherhood, but has
also stated he knows from a reliable source that Usch has
had a very intimate American friend who—as Usch
writes it—

would in his opinion be the father much more likely.
. . . When this news was related to me, I had
passed the whole scale of emotions and I could not
care what else people might think of to push me

129

further into hell. It is impossible to give an account of that time or of the reaction of my mother who is the personified code of moral.

But, Usch, who has given a briefer, better account of this old story that is older than any monument we ever went to see? And why must it be written after all this time? Why must she suffer all over again? Because, apart from some little incidents one gets used to, nothing has happened since the events in court until a week before the writing of this letter, when Usch goes to the office where all fatherless children are registered, and asks that now, after two years, the guardianship for her daughter be transferred officially to her. Then, suddenly, the bureaucratic mechanisms begin to grind—set in motion by caretaker clerks who inform her that everyone possibly concerned will now be questioned so that the case may be brought to a conclusion. She tries to convince these statisticians, these chronologists of sadness, that such an undertaking is useless and will help no one. But the mechanisms that have begun inexorably to grind, grind on—

. . . and since it is impossible to stop the machinery, I must apologize if perhaps now after all this time someone might ask whether you ever knew a girl named Ursula Müller. I cannot put it into words how terrible I feel, please, be not too angry with me.

Ah, Usch . . . Usch. Angry with you? I who have nothing but pleasant memories of Europe, as if life were scenery taken in Kodachrome? Angry with you? Usch, I can hardly wait to get my hands on paper.

"My dear Usch," I begin, but beyond that point I cannot go. What shall I say? Shall I tell her of my sadness at her tale? Shall I tell her that I hope she will be happy once again? Shall I tell her that if I ever return to Europe I will come to visit her? I am full of conflict. I can't bear to see this story concluded, but neither can I lift a finger to keep it going. Each time I sit with pen in hand, I find myself supposing. Suppose, for example, I had not been transferred so abruptly to the Pfalz. Or suppose, that final evening in Bad Cannstatt, I had said I could go to Berlin with her in August. Suppose I had taken another perspective toward those moist blue eyes. Ah, suppose a million things—the past is past—and still I go on supposing. Orlando D'Ampezza, for instance, he sticks in my throat like a fishbone. But he is not the only "heavy" in this sad tale. Certainly it was not Orlando who refused to interpret, one summer night, the meaning in a pair of misty eyes; not he who, blinded with a kaleidoscopic vision that would better have been found between the covers of a *National Geographic*, urged the girl to go to Italy, where the scenery's so beautiful. Well, at this rate, one could have himself sharing paternity for the population explosion of the world.

Meanwhile, as I sit supposing, the months go by, and I receive another letter from Ursula. Included is a color photograph of her daughter, Sigrid. She is a beautiful child who, except for a head of lush black curls, looks exactly like her mother. In the letter itself, which is quite short, Usch speculates on my silence, wonders if I have disapproved, and assures me that all is well. "We must

131

not be sorry for anything that happened or not happened in the past," she writes. "This time, too, is part of our lives, it probably was necessary as anything that forms ourselves." And then, toward the end of the letter, she informs me that she has gotten married. Her husband is a university student, and, as she puts it, "though I had not fallen desperately in love as one usually terms such happenings, I have found in Otto a good comrade, who, which was the most important thing, loves little Sigrid and is already her favorite and competent authority."

As it happens, I myself have gotten married during the interval, and this event, in light of Usch's, surely provides me with strong motive to cease my procrastination and write the letter I have been trying so long to write. Well, one of these days I am probably going to write it. I've an idea it won't be so difficult now. For one thing, I have stopped supposing. About the past, anyway. Lately, I find myself dreaming a daydream about Ursula. It pops into my head at the oddest moments. It began when my wife suggested not long ago that we take our vacation in Europe next year. I keep thinking—wouldn't it be nice if we could all get together in Berlin? I even have a vision. There am I with my svelte American wife, and there is Usch, more ample than ever now, and little Sigrid, the Teutonic bambino, and this husband, Otto, who's such a good companion. We're coming down the Kurfürsten-damm, strung out across the sidewalk in a gay line, arms linked, with the child gamboling on ahead. We're walking out toward you implausibly, as in the finale of a heart-warming movie—a dream ending.

The Toll

If it had not been for force of habit, Henry Wilson would not have been so sure, afterward, of having paid the correct amount of toll, but, as always before driving into the city, he bought gas at a filling station near his country house, took a quarter from the change handed him by the attendant, and placed it on the seat beside him so that when he reached the toll booths on the expressway he would not have to disengage his safety belt and fish in his pocket for coins. Fifty minutes later, tooling along the expressway beneath the hot noonday sun of July, Wilson passed a large green sign that warned drivers to reduce speed for the toll plaza ahead, and, easing his foot off the gas pedal, felt the car begin to slow down. At forty miles an hour, he entered the plaza, where the three lanes of the expressway bellied into six lanes that entered gateways between rows of concrete-and-glass toll booths, and removed his foot entirely from the accelerator. When his speedometer read thirty miles an hour, he shifted into second gear, headed for an exact-change lane on the far left-hand side of the plaza, and reached for the quarter on the seat; then, holding the quarter and the steering wheel in his right hand, he rolled down the window beside him with his left hand, entered the gateway, and drew up alongside the toll booth and its change hopper—a funnel-shaped wire basket hanging below a bull's-eye target plate that had been installed by the turnpike authorities as a coy reminder to drivers to be careful about aiming their coins. Disdaining the bull's-eye target, Wilson pulled his car very close to the basket, switched the quarter to his left hand, and dropped it into the mouth of the hopper. Afterward, still in second gear, he applied gentle pressure to the gas pedal and allowed the car to edge forward as he waited for the red light beyond the booth to change to green. The light, however, remained unaccountably red.

Wilson brought his car to a stop, glanced right and left around him, but saw no one. Almost at once a pall of heat rebounding off the asphalt surface of the plaza flooded through the open windows, causing a trickle of sweat to run over his forehead and into his eyes. Blinking, Wilson looked into his rear-vision mirror and saw several other vehicles coming up behind him; then, putting the car into gear, he started slowly toward the red light. As he drew abreast of it, he heard shouts, looked back over his shoulder, and saw a uniformed toll collector emerge, waving his arms, from the rear of the booth, but because the man was partially obscured by heat waves shimmering off the asphalt and by a cloud of blue exhaust fumes that hung over the plaza, Wilson assumed that he was being told to keep going, and drove on past the light. When the shouts were redoubled, however, he pulled his car over to one side, parked it, and unfastened his safety belt. Then he climbed out into the stunning light of the sun, which, combined with the deafening roar of traffic passing through the gateway and the acrid stench of exhaust fumes, made him suddenly dizzy. For a moment Wilson felt as if he had stepped into another world. The awful heat even seemed to have distorted the shadow of a flagpole and limp banner surmounting the roof of the toll booth so that it looked like a glob of wax melting down over the side of a candle. Now, with slow, disoriented steps, Wilson walked toward the toll collector and found himself confronting a bulky, middle-aged man who was wearing the kind of sunglasses worn by motorcycle policemen.

"What's the matter?" he asked.

"What's the matter?" echoed the toll collector with amazement. "What's the matter with going through a red light?"

"I thought you were waving me on," Wilson said calmly.

"Why should I wave you on?" replied the toll collector. "You haven't paid your quarter."

"Certainly I paid a quarter. That's why I assumed you were waving me on."

"Whatever you put in there couldn't have been a quarter," said the toll collector, shaking his head. "If you'd paid a quarter, the light would've changed to green."

"Listen, I *know* I paid a quarter," Wilson said. "I'm positive of it."

The toll collector, who was sweating profusely in the midday heat, ran the sleeve of his shirt across his forehead in an eloquent gesture of discomfort and despair. "So is everybody," he murmured. "But the machine is positive you didn't."

"Well, the machine is wrong," Wilson replied.

"How many times a day d'you think people tell me that?" said the toll collector with a smirk, and, grimacing up at the broiling sun, went back into the cubicle, where he sat down upon a stool beside a metal sluiceway that dropped into a coin intake box.

Wilson followed him as far as the doorway. "I'm not interested in what other people tell you," he said stiffly. "The fact is I have paid my toll."

"Can you prove it?" the toll collector asked in a bored tone of voice.

"Can you prove I didn't?"

"I don't have to," the toll collector replied, holding up a piece of paper upon which he had written the registration number of Wilson's car. "The machine has already done that. All I have to do is turn over your number to the authorities."

This nonchalant reply was extremely annoying to Wilson, but he was careful not to show it. Instead, he took a deep breath and stuck his head into the booth, which was swollen with hot air, like a jar at the end of a blowpipe. "The proof that I paid the correct amount is that I just didn't reach into my pocket at random for change," he said. "I had already selected a quarter and put it on the seat beside me when I bought gas. For this reason, I'm positive it was a quarter I dropped into the basket."

"Positive," the toll collector repeated, with no attempt to hide his disbelief. "How can you be positive it wasn't a nickel?"

"Haven't I just told you?" Wilson exclaimed, taking a step into the stifling booth. "From the moment I received change from the filling-station attendant, I had to handle the quarter too often to make such a mistake. I had to transfer it from my left hand to my right hand to the seat, and then back again before I dropped it into the—" Wilson broke off as he realized that he was accompanying his explanation with a series of exaggerated gestures whose ludicrous aspect could not fail to be appreciated by the toll collector. And, in addition to this, he was suddenly ashamed of the fussy ritualistic aspect of the actions he had described. My whole defense rests upon stodgy habit, he thought with dismay, and gasped for air in the incredible heat.

The toll collector was quick to interpret the implications of Wilson's silence. "I'm surprised you can't remember whether it was a George Washington quarter or a liberty head," he observed. "Besides, how can this story of yours mean anything to me? Just take a look at the light. Why, since you've been standing here, it's changed for at least half a dozen people!"

With a sinking feeling Wilson glanced through the window of the booth and saw the red light change to green to permit passage of a car. Then, looking at the sluiceway beyond the toll collector's stool, he saw several coins glinting as they slid into the machine, which received them with a click that was immediately reflected by still another change of the light. For a moment he was

137

filled with doubt. Was it possible that he had been mistaken all along? In this mood, the heat became doubly oppressive.

The toll collector seemed to be reading Wilson's mind. "How could the machine be wrong for you and not for all these others?" he asked triumphantly. "The fact is the machine is working perfectly. It's weighing quarters, nickels, and combinations of nickels and dimes—whatever adds up to twenty-five cents, excepting pennies, of course, which are not allowed."

"Isn't it possible that my quarter could have fallen into the machine in such a way that the device didn't properly trigger its signal to the stop light?" Wilson asked, but without conviction. He thought about leaving, but the heat, acting upon him like a soporific, had begun to make him drowsy.

"Anything is possible," the toll collector responded with a yawn. "I'm not being paid, however, to consider remote possibilities."

"No, you're being paid to assume that the machine is infallible," Wilson said.

"Look at the machine," the toll collector intoned with a sigh as the last of several cars passed through the gateway without incident.

"The hell with the machine," Wilson replied, but, tiring of the argument, he wondered if he should not just pay another quarter and be on his way.

"Listen, I don't like the machine any more than you do," the toll collector replied. "I can tell you it's no fun sitting here in this heat, listening to silver rattle through a slot. I'd rather be in one of the manned collection booths any day of the week, but we have to spot-check these exact-change lanes because of what some people'll do to chisel the state out of a lousy two bits. You'd be amazed at the collection of junk they fish out of these boxes. Why, they fill whole satchels full of washers with the holes taped over, metal punchings from factories, foreign coins from countries you never heard of, pennies that have been weighted by rimming them with copper rings from spark plugs, sawed-off key heads, and even religious medals!"

"Since you've brought up the subject of chiseling, why don't you open the machine and check it to see if my coin was good or bad?" Wilson replied.

"I can't do that!" said the toll collector, as if scandalized by the suggestion. "It's not allowed by the authorities. Besides, by the time I got someone with authority to come over here to open the box, I'd be hauled on the carpet for having blocked up a lane."

"So you are merely a guardian for a machine whose absolute judgments cannot be contradicted," Wilson said.

"It's a job," the toll collector replied. "Like any other."

"Some job," Wilson said. "Playing flunkey to a machine."

There was a moment of silence; then the toll collector shrugged and, pulling his soaked shirt front from his chest with thumbs and forefingers, made it flutter up and down. "There's no need to be insulting," he said in a conciliatory tone of voice. "It's not so bad a job as you seem to think. I only have to pull duty on the exact-change lanes once a week, which means I spend four days in one of the manned collection booths, where there are certain compensations."

"Compensations?" Wilson echoed.

"Well, one thing is, I collect coins."

Wilson barely suppressed a laugh. "Yes, yours is a redundant profession, all right," he observed.

"Don't knock it," said the toll collector solemnly. "The 1971 D dime is worth ten dollars these days. The D means it was minted in Denver, and it's valuable on account of a limited circulation of only three hundred thousand. The dime to look for, though, is the 1942 that was struck over the '41. During wartime there was a shortage of silver, so they had to alter a certain number of coins from the previous year in order to make up a new issue. That one's worth thirty dollars, but it's awfully rare. I've only come across a couple of them in the whole eight years I've been on this job."

Wilson found himself touched by the fact that the toll collector had managed to pursue a hobby in the confines of his cubicle, for it gave the man the human dimension that seemed to be lacking in him. Now, as if to ameliorate his previous harsh pronouncements, Wilson reached into his pocket and, withdrawing his change, examined the solitary dime that was contained in it. "Nothing but a 1957 Roosevelt," he announced.

"Worthless," the toll collector replied, shifting his bulk on the stool as he watched several more coins tumble down the sluiceway and into the collection box. "You know, it's hard to sit here watching all that silver slide by without being able to examine it," he said disconsolately. "I mean to think there may be a fortune in rare coins going past me. I can tell you I'll be glad when they install electric cameras on these exact-change lanes. That way the chiselers will have their license numbers recorded automatically."

"Automatically," said Wilson, who was only half listening, for the heat had rendered him totally listless.

"And that's not all," the toll collector went on. "One of these days, mark my words, the machine will be given a built-in capacity to deal with violators—some kind of special ray, probably, that'll shut off their ignitions and keep 'em stalled until they fork over."

"Some idea," Wilson said, smiling in spite of himself. "When that happens, you'll be able to spend five days a week on the manned collection lanes."

"I won't mind a bit," the toll collector replied. "Especially on days like today. Why, you wouldn't believe the sights women give you in this kind of heat! I mean it's a regular hit parade of open blouses, unbuttoned halters, and skirts hiked up—not to mention how some of these couples carry on!" Now, panting in the stifling heat, the toll collector broke into an ocean of perspiration. A moment later he ostentatiously crumpled up the piece of paper bearing the registration number of Wilson's car and dropped it on the floor; then, lifting himself off his stool, he leaned toward Wilson, ducked his head as if to ward off a barrage of flesh, and told breathlessly of taking money from hands whose blandly hidden counterparts supported crouched and squirming girls. "And don't think I don't know how to take my own good time making change!" he shouted.

Staring into the convex lenses of the toll collector's sunglasses, Wilson saw a grotesquely distorted and bloated reflection that seemed to be not so much a reflection of his own face as a caricature of the toll collector's senselessly vicarious lust, and started for the doorway.

The toll collector moved his bulk with surprising speed, however, and blocked the exit. "Listen, I really envy you going into the city," he said, giving his head a shake of genuine regret. "Why, if what I see passing through here is an indication, that town must be a regular summer paradise!"

This is one very bored and lonely toll collector, Wilson thought, and, glancing at the crumpled piece of paper on the floor, wondered if his presence had not become the price of it. "I have to be getting on," he said.

"Don't hurry away," the toll collector replied. "I've got a jug of cold lemonade."

The idea of drinking the toll collector's lemonade filled Wilson with disgust. Already repelled by the lonely voyeuristic prattle, he had no inclination at all to accept the hospitality the man now insisted upon tendering in his absurd cubicle of glass and concrete. It was as if he had been importuned to pay a bribe. "No thanks," he said shortly, and took a half step toward the door.

The toll collector made no effort to move, but simply stood in the way, fluttering his stained shirt front with feminine indolence. "Why the sudden rush?" he asked in a wounded tone.

Wilson looked at him with distaste. "Please get out of the doorway," he said.

"What?" the toll collector cried, his mouth dropping open with astonishment. "What kind of a way is that to talk? And, besides, aren't you forgetting something?"

"Forgetting something . . . ?"

"Your toll," said the toll collector with an ominous smirk. "You still haven't paid your toll."

Wilson looked at the man with loathing and saw that the large pair of sunglasses, which at first glance had seemed to lend his face an impassive look of authority, merely accentuated a weak mouth that, even while delivering words of warning, trembled upon the brink of recrimination. "I have no intention of paying you or that damn machine of yours anything," he said.

"Who d'you think you are?" the toll collector shouted in a voice that was shrill with rage. "First you come in here pleading about your toll; then you butter me up to get me to let you off and confide all kinds of things to you; and now you think you're just going to up and leave without paying?"

"For the last time," Wilson said evenly, "get out of my way."

With these words, Wilson attempted to shoulder his way through the exit, but the toll collector put up surprisingly strong resistance to this effort and, closing his arms around Wilson's chest, held him fast. A moment later, locked in a heavy, awkward embrace, the two men were swaying back and forth in the choking hot confines of the cubicle. To begin with, Wilson felt a kind of amused detachment for the ludicrous aspect of the struggle he was engaged in, but then, suddenly, the glare of the sun glinting off the toll plaza and the overwhelming heat inside the booth conspired to fill him with the horror of suffocation. With an immense effort born of fear and rage, he broke the toll collector's grip and flung the man to the other side of the cubicle, where, stumbling over the stool and the coin collection box, he fell heavily against a wall and slumped to the floor. For an instant every nerve in Wilson's body urged him to flee, but he was too exhausted from the struggle to do anything except lean against the side of the open doorway. Now, breathing heavily, he was relieved to see his adversary stir, sit up, and begin to rub his shoulder.

"What'd you have to do that for?" the toll collector whined. "That was just plain foolish."

"You had no right to block my way," Wilson answered.

"No right!" the toll collector exclaimed. "Here I am— a man in uniform—and you tell me I have no right. The trouble with your kind is you have no respect."

"Good luck with your dimes," Wilson said scornfully, and stepped out of the booth into the shattering noise, awful heat, and choking fumes of the toll plaza.

"Don't forget I still have your registration number," the toll collector called plaintively after him.

"So long," Wilson said, and started for his car. So long, gateman to paradise, he thought. All you need in that caldron is a Doberman pinscher named Cerberus . . .

"I'm warning you for the last time . . ."

Wilson looked back and saw that the toll collector, who was still rubbing his shoulder, had taken a few steps out of the booth, as if he were debating whether to try again to detain him. The poor devil is so lonely he must want to flag down everybody, Wilson thought.

"If I turn in your number, you'll be in a lot of trouble!"

Without reply, Wilson climbed into his car, switched on the engine, and started away. The toll collector isn't going to turn in my number, he told himself, and, glancing into his rear-vision mirror, saw the man pop several times in and out of the booth, as if he were in the throes of some terrible indecision. "A bird in a cuckoo clock," Wilson said aloud, and shuddered involuntarily at the thought of the toll collector sitting out the rest of the scorching day in the exact-change cubicle, where, prevented from pursuing his hobbies of voyeurism and numismatics, he would be confined to coining sexual fantasies. But when the bulky figure had disappeared from view, Wilson found himself assailed by the uneasy feeling that he had paid too high a price for being right. He felt sorry for the toll collector, and he regretted what had taken place in the booth, but he also wondered if the man, after trying to forget his bruised shoulder with dreams of obtaining a rare coin or a forbidden glimpse of thigh, would not become sufficiently bored with his solitude to retrieve and uncrumple the piece of paper bearing the registration number and contact the authorities, who, outraged at Wilson's flouting of their machine and its lecherous guardian, would then contrive to track him down. For this reason he continued to glance into his rear-vision mirror, as if to assure himself that he was not being followed. There was nothing following him, however, except an inexorable stream of traffic flowing toward the city, whose skyline soon appeared in the distance, where, obscured by a ghostly combination of heat and smog, it loomed like a mirage. Wilson pressed his foot down upon the accelerator, and sped on hopefully toward its promise of anonymity.

145

A War Story

This is one of those stories that, for reasons of honor, have had to be suppressed. The principal characters are my brother and I and a brigadier general, and the plot concerns a bombardment, blackmail, and bribery. The story can now be told, because the general, who was responsible for the bombardment and for bribing my brother, has surely retired, or gone off to whatever Valhalla exists for generals, or been elevated, like so many of his confreres, to the presidency of some corporation, and my brother, who blackmailed the general—well, he was only eight years old at the time.

It was the summer of 1942, and our family had made its annual migration from Boston to a rented cottage on Duxbury Beach, some forty miles south of the city. My father came down only on weekends, because of gas rationing; my mother spent her days at the cottage tending my infant sister; and my brother and I, clad in bathing suits that had faded and dwindled into ragged loincloths, roamed freely from morning until night. The beach was a sandbar peninsula seven miles long, with the ocean on one side and Duxbury Bay on the other, and, except for a few summer people in the cottages near the mainland and some Coast Guardsmen out at Gurnet Point, it was uninhabited. A dirt road that ended at the cottage colony and a wooden bridge that rambled across the bay on piles, a mile farther along the peninsula, were the only routes of access. On Saturdays and Sundays picnickers came over the bridge and spread themselves upon the sand, but during the week the beach was deserted.

Like all boys at the seashore, my brother and I were beachcombers. We poached quahogs, collected driftwood, captured minnows trapped in tidal pools, and filled gunny sacks with pop bottles left behind by picnickers. But, above all else, we considered ourselves patriots. We salvaged tinfoil for the war effort from discarded cigarette packages, helped local residents dry sea moss to collect nitrates for munitions makers, and used the pop-bottle refunds to buy Victory stamps at the post office. In all these endeavors our relationship was a military one. Since I was two years the elder, I was a captain; my brother was a trusty scout. With the country at war, leadership and discipline were accepted as a matter of course, and, like a good soldier, my brother submitted to his status without complaint.

The war affected us in many ways that summer. There was a strict blackout every night, and when we went outside before bedtime, the unaccustomed darkness and the profound sea made us feel close and vulnerable to the

148

conflict. Wreckage washed ashore from ships sunk by U-boats, and each day we poked through fresh piles of debris, vaguely aware that we were examining the flotsam of catastrophe. The grownups talked incessantly of a submarine that had surfaced off the shore during World War I and lobbed a few shells into the marshland behind the beach. Had the Germans been aiming at the old cable station? Would they try again? And would they not send a landing party this time? The speculation of our elders filled us with delicious tension. The tin cans my brother and I were forever tossing into the waves became submarines, and the rocks we threw at them depth charges, and the constant vigil we maintained for flotsam, pop bottles, and marine life took on a new dimension. For now we were patrolling a stretch of the coast—a strategic flank of the republic.

It was with this lofty mission in mind that we arose at sunup one weekday morning in July, made ourselves breakfast, and, taking our bows and arrows, set off along the beach for our favorite position of defense, an abandoned duck-hunting camp that lay hidden in the dunes several miles beyond the old bridge and almost halfway out to Gurnet Point. The camp was a rambling frame-and-tarpaper affair, upon which time and the elements had wrought a deceptive camouflage. Winds and winter storms had so shifted the dunes that it was nearly buried. Foxtail and beach-plum bushes had taken root in sand covering the rooftop, and only in a hollow on the leeward side was any part of the building visible. Here my brother and I had torn away some rotted boards and fashioned an entrance.

The interior of the camp was cavernous and dank. It consisted of four rooms, three of which were half filled with sand that had sifted down through cracks in the roof. In the largest room there were several bunks with mildewed mattresses, a rusted iron stove, some overturned chairs, and a long table. For us, these were the furnishings of a bunker from which we operated against the foe, and on this day, as on all the others, my brother and I played tirelessly at the same game. Captain and scout, we lay on the summit of a high dune, waiting to ambush enemy saboteurs who were disembarking from their rubber boats. When they came into range, we unleashed a hail of arrows at them. Then we retreated to the invisible fastness of our fort and hid until they stumbled, with Teutonic stupidity, into our line of fire, giving us an opportunity to decimate them with a volley fired through apertures in the rotting planks. Fierce struggles took place as the last fanatic attackers breached our bastion. It was hand-to-hand for more than an hour, and we backed slowly into a corner, each forefinger a revolver that barked incessantly. Suddenly I whirled and fired at a gigantic German who was climbing down through a hole in the roof. The Nazi fell, draped grotesquely over a beam. With my jackknife I administered a *coup de grâce.* And then my brother shouted an incredible thing. "You're dead!" he said to me. "You're shot!"

It was a forbidden stage direction in our game. I turned on him. "I'm not!" I replied. "I'm only grazed."

"No," said my brother gravely. "You're dead."

I struck him.

What followed was the story of all our quarrels. My

brother, hurt and outraged, began to cry, and, angry and ashamed, I called him a crybaby. "You're not a soldier," I said. It was the worst insult of all.

"I'm going to tell Father," he announced, weeping.

It was a threat that always restored the balance of power between us. "I'll never take you on patrol again," I told him, but the retort was uneasy.

"You'll get a spanking," my brother said.

I put my arm around him. "Here," I said. "You can use my jackknife in the next battle."

The knife was a prized possession. My brother stopped crying, but he threw my arm off his shoulder and walked away. Then he wiped his eyes and looked at the knife. "Why do I always have to be a scout?" he said bitterly. "Why can't I be a captain, too?"

I was amazed. My brother had never objected to his subordinate position before. I told him he was too young and too small to be a captain. "Anyway, you're always running to Father," I said scornfully. Then, seeing that he was about to cry again, I offered to let him use my bow as well as the knife for the next battle.

"No," he said. "I'm going home." And with that, he started for the doorway—a doorway no longer clogged with the bodies of our dead enemies.

A strange and terrifying thing happened next. My brother—a small, sad figure—paused before going out alone into the sunlight. He was hoping that I would call him back, and clearly it was up to me to make another overture. But before I could, there was the sound of a low-flying airplane, and then a tremendous explosion. The floor shuddered beneath us. The old beams quivered.

Sand and debris rained down upon us. My brother ran to my side and hid his face against my chest. There was another explosion, and another, in rapid succession. Part of the roof caved in, and the air became filled with the dust of decayed wood. We began to choke. Finally, in blind panic, we groped our way outside to the dunes.

We were just in time to see a second plane. It flew low over the beach, perhaps a hundred feet above the water's edge, and as it drew abreast of us, three objects dropped from the belly. Almost at once three geysers of sand and water rose into the air and there were three explosions, which merged with the noise of the plane into a single roar. We threw ourselves upon the sand and watched the plane disappear over Gurnet Point. Then we heard another plane, and we began, frantically, to dig.

No foxhole was ever dug faster, and no soldiers ever melted more gratefully into the earth than did my brother and I. Hugging each other, we lay in the cool sand, sobbing yet fascinated by the roar of the planes and the noise and spectacle of the bombs. From time to time we looked longingly down the beach in the direction of our cottage, but what we could see there only terrified us more, for the sand was crawling with tanks, trucks, and men, and an endless line of vehicles was creeping across the old wooden bridge.

"Maybe it's the Germans—" my brother began, in a quavering voice, but just then the planes returned for another run, and we pressed our faces into the sand.

For a long time after the planes went away, we remained in our foxhole. Then we got to our feet and started down the beach toward the bridge. There didn't seem to be anything else to do. We walked slowly, holding hands.

"If they're Germans, will they shoot us?" my brother asked.

"No," I replied. "We're too small." Somehow, it was the most comforting and tragic admission I had ever been forced to make.

As we drew closer to the bridge, we could make out squads of soldiers running to and fro with sandbags and shovels. A city of tents was being erected on the sand, and howitzers were being set in place behind the dunes. At the outskirts of the encampment we passed a huge sign that bore the words "DANGER—EXPLOSIVES" and that warned all unauthorized persons to stay out of an ordnance testing area. We knew, by now, that the soldiers were not the enemy but our own. It was a reassuring revelation, but soon we had new cause for anxiety, for as we entered the bivouac area a great silence fell over that part of the beach. Drivers stopped their trucks and leaned out of the cabs. Men dropped their work to look. It seemed that everyone was watching us. We walked even more slowly than before, until we came to a large tent— the largest tent of all.

A group of officers was standing before it. My brother and I stopped some yards short, and for a long moment we faced the officers and they faced us and nobody said a word. Finally, one of them, a colonel, came forward. "Well," he said. "Where have you boys come from?"

Too frightened to speak, I turned and pointed up the beach.

The colonel laughed, a trifle uneasily. *"Far* up the beach?" he asked.

"Where the bombs fell," said my brother shrilly.

The colonel stopped laughing. "Well," he said. "I think the general will want to hear about that." Placing one hand on my shoulder and one on my brother's, he herded us gently toward the tent.

It was easy to know who was the general. He was a tall man, with gray hair, blue eyes, a large stomach, and a grim face, and he held his hands on his hips the way our father did when making up his mind to mete out punishment. None of the other officers had their hands on their hips.

The colonel saluted the general, and spoke in a low, guarded voice, turning as he did so to point up the beach.

"Impossible!" the general snapped.

The colonel whispered something else.

The general nodded curtly and looked down at us. "How'd you get out there?" he demanded. It was more accusation than question.

"We walked," I said.

"When?" There was disbelief in the general's voice.

"This morning!" my brother shouted, in a tone of insulted integrity.

"How early this morning?" the general asked.

"When the sun came up," my brother replied triumphantly.

The general spun around and glared at his officers. "Was this beach cleared, or not?" he demanded.

Several of the officers protested that the beach had been carefully searched by patrols. The general said he'd like to know what kind of search could overlook two kids on a narrow strip of sand and dunes. No one answered him. "A pretty goddam sloppy search, gentlemen!" the general answered himself. Then he turned to us and asked if we had seen any patrols.

I shook my head.

"We were in our fort," my brother said.

Now the colonel bent down and smiled at my brother. "What kind of fort?" he asked.

"It isn't a fort," I said. "It's an old duck-hunting camp."

The colonel straightened and looked at the general. "Well, whatever it is," he said, "it certainly isn't on the maps, sir."

The general shook his head in disgust. There was a long whispered conference, and several times I could hear the colonel saying something about newspapers, publicity, and investigations. Finally the general called for silence with an irritable wave of his hand. "Tell them to run along home," he said.

"Can we ride in a jeep?" asked my brother, who was by now admiring the profusion of vehicles and equipment.

The colonel smiled. "We're very busy, young man," he said.

"Maybe we could help dig dugouts," my brother suggested.

"You just run along home now," the colonel said.

"We want to be soldiers," my brother persisted.

The colonel had started to walk away, but now he turned and looked at us. For some moments he was silent. Then he told us that soldiering was a very serious business, and that if we were to become soldiers we would

155

have to keep secret everything we had seen and heard
out at the duck-hunting camp. We promised that we
would. The colonel went over to the general, and there
was another conference, during which the general got red
in the face.

"What d'you think I'm running here?" he exploded
finally. "A combat exercise or a goddam country day
school?" It was hard to tell whom he was speaking to, because he started out addressing the colonel and wound up
looking at my brother and me.

The colonel and my brother and I flinched in unison.
Then an expression of deep hurt appeared on my brother's face, and it seemed as if he were about to cry again.
"I'm going to tell Father," he said softly. He was struggling for control, but it was the same tone of voice with
which he had threatened me out at the camp.

There was a moment of absolute silence, broken only
by the cries of gulls wheeling overhead and the gentle
rumble of waves upon the beach. The general turned
slowly and looked down at my brother, and I have often
thought since then that if he ever afterward had the occasion to demand the unconditional surrender of any of
the country's enemies, he was certainly a general who
understood the full meaning of what he asked. There was
another conference with the colonel, who announced to
us, a few moments later, that he would personally escort
us home and that we would indeed ride in a jeep.

"Can I wear a helmet?" my brother asked.

The colonel smiled weakly, removed his helmet, and
placed it upon my brother's head. The rim of the helmet
came down below his mouth. His next words were muf-

fled, but not inaudible. "Can we come back and be soldiers?"

"Can the general be sure you'll keep our secret?" the colonel asked.

He put the question with considerable gravity, and my brother and I gravely assured him of our silence. And so our tongues were bound with a seal of honor that neither of us would have dreamed of violating.

The colonel looked at the general, who said nothing, but shut his eyes and appeared to hold his breath. Then the colonel nodded, and said we'd better get started for home.

When we drove up to the cottage, our mother was standing on the porch, holding our baby sister. The colonel and my brother and I climbed out of the jeep and advanced over the sand to the porch, but before any of us could say anything, our mother said, "I've been worried about you. Where were you during those explosions?"

"In a bunker," my brother replied.

"Goodness," said our mother. She looked at the colonel. "I hope the boys haven't been in the way."

The colonel said with a gay smile that, quite the contrary, on behalf of the officers and men of the 104th Infantry Regiment, 26th National Guard Division, he had come to ask her permission to adopt us as mascots for the duration of the maneuvers.

Our mother said she thought that was awfully kind of the officers and men of the 104th Infantry Regiment and, since it was almost lunchtime, wouldn't the colonel like to step inside for a cup of coffee and a sandwich?

"We want to eat with the soldiers," said my brother.

"That's right!" the colonel said immediately. "All soldiers have to eat at the mess." He grinned at our mother
and shifted his feet in the sand.

"Aren't you lucky boys?" our mother said to us, beaming.

During the week that followed, my brother and I lived
all the dreams we had ever played, and some that we had
never even dreamed. We dug foxholes, went out on
patrol, waved signal flags, stood inspection, and walked
guard. Occasionally the soldiers took us on jeep rides and
gave us equipment. In addition to the helmet, which was
constantly on his head, my brother wore a poplin shirt
that reached almost to his knees, and a cartridge belt
around his waist, from which hung a water canteen, a
first-aid kit, and an empty bayonet scabbard.

We saw the general frequently. He was a ubiquitous
overseer, making constant inspections and supervising
even the most routine operations. Officers and men
seemed to spend as much time watching for and frantically signaling his approach as they did in preparing
for the business of war. My brother and I shared the common apprehension, and whenever the general appeared in
our vicinity we jumped to our feet with the others, and
my brother always rendered him a smart salute. The
general never spoke to my brother, and my brother, in
turn, never spoke to him. But two or three times I saw the
general look in our direction with a kind of curious disbelief.

Finally the day came when the regiment decamped.
The last tents were struck, and a long line of soldiers gave
the beach a final policing. Then the tanks, trucks, and

jeeps were lined up in a column, with the general's jeep, flying the divisional pennant, at the front. My brother and I stood at the end of the bridge, where the column would pass, watching in silence and sorrow. At the last moment the colonel came and told us that we could keep all the equipment we had acquired. He also reminded us that, being soldiers and veterans now, we would be bound to our promise forever. Then he shook hands with us and walked back and climbed into the jeep beside the general.

A moment later there was a shouted command, which was echoed down the line, and the procession got under way. When the general's jeep passed us, my brother squared his shoulders and saluted. The general, grim and unsmiling as always, returned the salute, and for one brief moment their eyes met in a glance that seemed to signify understanding of each other's motives and intent. Then the convoy rattled over the old wooden bridge and on to God only knows how many other beaches.

My brother and I started home, and as we walked I put my arm around his shoulder. It was not a protective gesture now, but one of respect. Something had changed between us, and from that day on, for the rest of our childhood, in all our games and enterprises, we were partners of equal rank.

The Proposal

Arthur Braden lay on the bed, with his hands clasped behind his neck, staring up at the ceiling. He had regretted his words the moment they were out, especially the self-consciously jocular manner with which he had uttered them, with which, in spite of himself, he had managed to fashion them into an expression that was hastily defensive—almost a wisecrack. Now, wondering what Valerie was thinking, he raised himself on his elbow and looked through the rear window of the motel cottage and across a field, lined on either side by woods, that rolled down to the edge of the Penobscot. The river flowed deep blue beneath the clear October sky, and the water looked very cold. Until she had averted them, Valerie's blue eyes had also looked cold, as if they had suddenly been veiled with a skim of ice—the first ice congealing on a pond. What a stupid way to tip your hand, Arthur reflected, but he knew that all summer long he had been on the edge of it,

161

like a car teetering perilously between macadam and a soft shoulder.

"Isn't this a lovely place?" she had cried, as soon as the motel owner had left them alone.

"Sure," said Arthur agreeably, flopping on the bed. "It's a regular honeymoon house."

"Let's do something exciting. Let's make a picnic and eat it down by the river."

"Let's get married," Arthur had replied. Now he realized that he had spoken almost without thinking, in an unguarded moment.

Valerie was still bustling about the tiny kitchen alcove, peering into cupboards, opening drawers, and unpacking and putting away groceries they had bought at a supermarket in Camden. As always, she appeared to be totally absorbed by what was closest at hand, only her present absorption seemed more profound than usual. Arthur decided that it was probably a reserve induced by his ill-timed remark. For some moments he studied her (she had begun to make sandwiches and she was licking some mayonnaise from her fingertips), noting with satisfaction the curved line where her Italian slacks stretched over her hips, and pondering at the same time how unbelievably graceful she was in performing even the homeliest, most housewifely gestures. Yet was it not at these moments—precisely at these tranquil moments when they seemed a part of some soft domestic tableau—that they had, over the year they had known each other, inevitably quarreled? Arthur wondered if this was because each of them felt that getting married would disrupt the delicious balance between domesticity and license that was inherent in their liaison. Though he tried to consider the prospect impassively, however, he could not dispel a slight feeling of annoyance, which he was bound to recognize as the purest male chauvinism, that this view of their affair should, in all likelihood, be hers as well as his. (She was, after all, twenty-seven, no matter how independent she pretended to be.) But the question of her age—the idea that it should somehow be especially meaningful to her —became ambiguous when placed in the context of the year they had been together, and, faced with this impasse, Arthur suddenly found himself considering a welter of tiny contradictions about Valerie. He remembered, for example, that as they had come over the walk to the cottage with the proprietor, she had skipped happily along beside him, using the sleeves of her suede jacket as a muff against the chill late-afternoon wind. Or had the gesture been motivated by some deeper practicality—a desire, perhaps, to provide camouflage for the naked fingers of her left hand? Tangled once again in the uncertainties of his thinking, Arthur was quite unprepared when Valerie decided to retrieve them from the long silence that had ensued his unfortunate lapse of judgment.

"While you were unloading the car, the owner told me about a lovely spot by the water's edge," she said. "He's built a boardwalk through the field so people can go down there without getting their feet wet in the grass."

"Sounds fine," replied Arthur absently.

"Wasn't he nice, and isn't this a nice cottage?"

"Affirmative times two," Arthur said.

"Sweetie, are you going to be in one of your laconic moods?"

"No," said Arthur, "it's just that I've already said too

much." He detested the shade of archness and evasion in his words, for he knew it inevitably led to sparring—the kind of sparring that could only end badly.

"I wonder if that's possible," Valerie murmured. "I mean to have already said too much."

Arthur put his head back on the pillow and looked up at the ceiling again. Round one, he thought, and the antagonists are circling each other warily. "You and I are chock full of integrity and independence," he told her. "We're not going down without a fight."

"Oh, Arthur, that's probably the whole trouble. We're afraid of sinking, or being submerged, or something."

"Who's afraid?" said Arthur to the ceiling. You're afraid, he reflected. But did he want to marry her all the more because he sensed she might refuse him? No, far too simple; he could not believe that it was merely a question of obtaining the assurance of concession. Was it true, then—partially true at least—that one wished to marry a woman only when it became apparent that she retained some secret reserve of fascination which, even beyond the sheerest intimacy, was not to be yielded up? Probably, Arthur decided. And, if so, the reverse was also true. The idea depressed him, for if it was Valerie's style and her enthusiasm for it that intrigued him, and if she did not find an equivalent reflection in her study of him—no, he could scarcely allow himself to conceive of that. Arthur followed the course of a faint crack in the ceiling and found himself trying to remember the words of the ultimatum he had composed and poised himself to deliver the night before—the first of their vacation. The motel in York was a bad choice (his choice), an idiot elfin's court of dollhouses with carnival trim, shadowy miniature verandas, and a total vulnerability to headlights and the sound of tires slapping over seams in the adjacent concrete highway. He had gone out late to mail a letter to some friends they were planning to visit in Connecticut on their way back to the city, and when he returned, ready to confront her, he had found her sitting up in bed, giggling, surrounded by a pile of covers and half a dozen electric heaters that she had filched from neighboring cabins, scattered about the room, and turned on full blast. "Oh, Arthur," she had said, profoundly disappointed at his disapproval. "You've got such a stuffy law-abiding streak." Did she mean no style? Arthur wondered, still following the crack that petered out in a far corner of the room.

Now he turned his head and watched her pour soup into a thermos bottle and pack sandwiches into a wicker picnic basket. "Maybe I should ask the man for extra heaters tonight," he said fondly.

"Oh, yes, do!" said Valerie. "Let's have our picnic and then come back and turn on all the heaters."

Half an hour later they were eating their sandwiches and sitting with their backs against the bank at the foot of the meadow. Between the meadow and the river's edge there was a stretch of shore, thirty or forty yards wide, that consisted of tens of thousands of round, burnished rocks, all of them approximately the size of tennis balls. The river flowed swiftly with the tide toward the sea, and the water looked very deep, especially now that the sun was setting.

Valerie was munching her sandwich and looking out across the river. "The rocky coast of Maine," she said. "How d'you suppose they got to be all of a size—the rocks?"

"Erosion," Arthur replied.

"But all of a size!"

"Aren't grains of beach sand all of a size?"

"I never thought about it," she replied with a tiny shiver. "Then someday this'll be a sandy beach?"

"Why not?" said Arthur.

"Mmm," Valerie said, biting deeply into her sandwich. "Yummy."

She was examining the marks her teeth had made in the bread, and, watching her, Arthur was filled with awe at her ability to switch her absorption momentarily from one thing to the next. I could watch her face forever, he thought. But he found himself looking at the plastic cups, empty now, from which they had drunk their soup. The cups sat beside the wicker basket at their feet—small and childlike and terribly misplaced in this sea of rocks which was slowly dissolving into sand. Arthur had a sudden urge to replace them in the basket; instead, he looked again at Valerie, who was staring across the dark water as if she had forgotten he was there. In this mood, the hollows beneath her eyes and her high cheekbones gave her face an appealing gravity. How sad it was to think that she—*they*—would grow old so much faster than and diminish just as inexorably as the rocks.

"I love you, Valerie," he said.

Abruptly, he got to his feet and started off on a short tour of the shore, throwing stones into the swift current

of the river, which swept the ripples toward the sea, even
as they disappeared. When he returned, he was carrying
a barrel stave and a badly pitted rubber ball that the tide
had left stranded upon the rocks. Valerie was lying on
her back, one arm stretched out, already nestling as if
for comfort among the aging pile. "Hey, wake up,"
Arthur said. "I'll hit some out to you."

She opened her eyes slowly; then, seeing the ball, she
jumped to her feet and ran gracefully out across the bed
of rocks, on her tiptoes, her arms flung wide to maintain
her balance.

"Farther!" Arthur shouted.

Paralleling the river, Valerie moved downstream.

"Farther!" he shouted and, throwing the ball into the
air, swiped viciously at it with the stave, and missed.
Again he tried, and again he missed. The ball dropped on
the rocks at his feet and bounced away. Arthur pursued
it, threw it into the air, and swung a third time. Valerie
was shouting at him through hands she had cupped to her
mouth, and now, seeing her smile, he was determined to
send the ball beyond her. Holding it between his thumb
and forefinger, he let it drop and swung at it, using only
his right hand on the stave. The ball sailed out, struck a
rock beside Valerie, and bounded high into the air. When
she retrieved it, she threw it in to him with fetching awk-
wardness. The ball landed short, midway between them,
and they started toward it.

"Two hands for beginners," Valerie said, when they
met. "I bet you can't hit it with two hands."

"Here, you try," he replied, handing her the stave and
the ball. But as he started running out across the rocks,

167

he was suddenly overwhelmed by a feeling of absurdity, knowing even before he turned to face her that their efforts in this childish game had already exceeded their capacity for it. He was relieved when, on the first swing, Valerie sent the ball out at an angle into the river, where it landed with a splash and, caught in the tidal current, coursed swiftly toward the sea.

"Bon voyage, little ball!" Valerie cried.

Hand in hand, they stood at the water's edge and watched the ball disappear. Then, all at once, Arthur felt her tremble and saw that her eyes had become veiled again, as if, looking into the deep water, she had suddenly imagined herself submerged in it.

"Let's go back to the cottage and have a drink," he said.

Leading her away from the water, he took the picnic basket, clambered up the bank to the meadow, and pulled Valerie up after him. They were walking through a stretch of tall grass toward the boardwalk when she pointed to a tiny path that cut across the field, parallel to the river, from the woods on either side.

"What's that?" she asked.

"That?" Arthur said. "That's a deer trail."

"How d'you know?"

He looked at her with fond amusement. "How do I know anything?" he said. "How do I know that grains of sand are all of a size?"

"A deer trail," Valerie said, and bent down to touch the bare ground where the track crossed at their feet. "I've never seen deer except from cars, and once from somebody's porch, when they were very far away. Where are they always?"

"They're hiding," Arthur said. "In the woods."

"But they made this trail!"

"At night," Arthur said.

"Why at night?"

"That's when they come out to feed," he told her. "They feel safer then."

"D'you think they'll come out tonight?"

"Sure," Arthur said. "They're probably watching us right now, waiting for us to leave."

"Arthur, what would we do if they came? Couldn't we hold our breath and stand very still?"

Arthur looked toward the woods that were dark on either side and filled with the dankness of river mist. "It would depend on the wind," he replied. "If we were downwind and if we were careful not to make any sudden movements, we might be able to crouch in the grass without being spotted."

"Oh, I wish we could see one!"

"We might have to stay for hours," said Arthur, taking her gently by the arm and leading her toward the boardwalk.

"Everything has to come out sometime," Valerie murmured, searching the woods as they returned to the cottage.

"You know," said Valerie—she was sitting in the opposite chair, leaning intently toward him, and balancing her drink on the armrest—"all this summer when I sensed you were going to ask me to marry you, all I kept thinking was what a fine, dandy time I was going to have turning you down."

"No kidding," Arthur said, but though he managed to

conceal it, he was surprised. "No kidding."

"And now that you've gone ahead and done it, I suppose I'm more scared than anything else. I mean I really don't feel hostility."

"Well, that's gratifying," said Arthur dryly.

"Harder and harder," she murmured. "You make a cult of it, Arthur. But is it rejection you're afraid of, or are you afraid I might not marry you?"

"Christ," Arthur said. "Everybody's afraid."

Valerie shut her eyes very tightly and winced as if she were trying to conjure up his face. "I'm afraid of living with you the way we're living now," she said. "I'm afraid of confronting you with my awful pride and you confronting me with yours and eternally opposing each other and making up in bed and then confronting each other again and again and again. I'm afraid of wanting to turn you down for some secret satisfaction that will break my heart in spite of it. Oh, Arthur, aren't you afraid of anything?"

He knew she was reaching out to him, and yet, finding himself torn only between addressing her either harshly or sentimentally, he could only try for calmness. "Yes, I'm afraid of one thing," he said flatly. "I'm afraid this little colloquy could go on forever. So I'm going to make it easier for you. I'm going to give you a time limit in which to make a decision. In fact, I'm going to give you exactly—" He was so immersed in the sequence of his words that he did not even have time to flinch. He saw just the briefest flash of the glass and her hand rising straight for his face, and the shining wall of liquid.

It astonished him how much the bourbon stung. He

was even afraid that he had been blinded, that the alcohol, like some corrosive acid, was irremediably searing his eyeballs. Gasping, he pressed his knuckles into the sockets; then he lowered his hands, opened his eyes, and, blinking back the tears which had begun to dilute his pain, saw that she was still leaning forward in her chair and that for some reason she had put on her sunglasses. Unaccountably now he reached down, righted the glass that had dropped from his hand to the floor, and began to retrieve the ice cubes (both his and hers) which lay upon the carpet. Cold, slippery, badly managed by his trembling fingers, the cubes dropped into the bottom of the glass with ludicrous, unnerving clinks that made a mockery of his deliberation. When he had picked up the last of them, he straightened slowly, saw at eye level the fingers with which she clenched her own empty glass, and, reaching out, struck her full across the face with the back of his hand.

Her reaction was so abrupt and furious that, afterward, he would not be able to remember its beginning. All he would remember was the struggle—a macabre dance, awful for its silence, in which they swayed back and forth across the room, he holding her at arm's length by the wrists, seeing distorted glimpses of his face in the dark convex circles of her sunglasses. Ludicrous, he kept thinking. Ludicrous . . .

"Control yourself," he said, shaking her.

She ceased struggling at once, and removed the sunglasses. "Oh, God!" she cried. "Oh, to think that I could ever touch *you!*"

He was on the verge of slackening his hold when she

171

lunged at him again, and, suddenly, sensing her despair, he was tired—tired and already disengaged. An icy calm descended over him. For a moment longer he contained her onslaught; then, using her wrists as levers, he flung her upon the bed, went to the window, and touched his forehead against a pane. Because he was breathing heavily, the glass began to cloud over at once with condensation. He knew that it was up to him to speak, but he could think of nothing to say—absolutely nothing—and when he heard the door open and close behind him, he felt only relief at being left alone. Now, through the misty window, he saw Valerie cross the lawn behind the cottage and start down through the meadow toward the river, where the water was shining black as anthracite in the last light of day. Outside, the evening chill was causing the spot of condensation to diminish rapidly from the pane. When it disappears entirely, I'll go after her, Arthur told himself, but long after the last trace of moisture had fled the polished surface, he was still standing at the window. By this time Valerie was out of sight—at the water's edge, no doubt. He thought of her standing alone amid the tens of thousands of stones that lined the shore at the edge of the black current sweeping toward the sea. But then he saw himself standing there, and he was filled with a fear that was not only a fear of being alone but also of being capable only of seeing himself alone. And, suddenly, he realized that he was looking no farther than the surface of the glass before his face, and that it was reflecting merely the faintest outline of his features, leaving all the rest without substance, in transparent shadow, to be imagined. . . .

172

Now, with a great effort, Arthur forced himself to look beyond the window, and even as he did, he saw the deer —three of them—emerge from the woods and start across the trail at the lower end of the field. Then he saw Valerie. She was crouching, as he had told her to crouch, in the tall grass at the foot of the boardwalk, and she was turning her face in his direction, turning again and again, as if imploring him to watch, but not daring to risk any further movement. Arthur left the window, hurried out of the cottage, and started down through the meadow. Tails twitching, ears erect, the deer—alarmed, afraid, forever anticipating danger—were passing into the trees on the other side as he came over the wooden planks of the boardwalk and stood at Valerie's side. Smiling up at him, her eyes filled with tears, she lifted a finger to her lips and turned away again. He nodded, following her gaze toward the grove where the deer could be heard milling softly out of sight, and finally, when the sounds of fright had sifted into silence, he bent down and touched her hair.

Angel of Death A
dam Foster was remov-
ing toadstools from the front yard of his weekend cottage when he heard his mother's car climbing the
driveway through the woods. The toadstools had first
appeared in isolated clumps in August; now, in September, after several heavy rainstorms, they were sprouting
everywhere. They were lumpy funguses with glabrous
yellowish caps and yellow gills. The stems were stumpy.
Some of the toadstools were moldy, others were rotting,
a few had dissolved into smears of black slime on the
grass. Adam was digging them out of the turf with a
spade, and tossing them into a bushel basket. He was doing this because he was afraid that little John, his fifteen-
month-old son, might tuck into one. The toadstools
looked ugly and poisonous, and there were dozens and
dozens of them in the tiny yard where the child played.
Moreover, some of the rotting ones gave off an acutely
pungent odor which Adam's wife, Margaret, had complained about.

When his mother's car came into view, Adam stuck his spade in the ground and walked across the yard. As he did, he called into the cottage to Margaret and told her to bring out the baby. His mother was smiling at him through the windshield. Her face was full of happiness and repose. There was not the slightest trace of fatigue in it. No one could have guessed that she had just driven two hundred and fifty miles. Adam opened the door for her, helped her out of the car, and kissed her on the cheek. His mother smiled and, for a brief moment, held his face between her hands. Then Margaret and little John came out of the cottage. The baby, all joy and pride at his recently achieved mobility, wobbled across the yard. Adam called encouragement. Mrs. Foster bent down and spread her arms wide.

"Oh, precious!" she exclaimed. "How well he walks! How wonderful to be here!"

Enthralled by the sight and color of a new car, the baby ambled past her and began beating a tattoo on a fender with tiny hands.

Mrs. Foster straightened up as Margaret approached. The two women kissed.

"Did you have a good trip?" Margaret asked.

"I had a lovely trip," Mrs. Foster replied. "I went through valley after valley where the trees were beginning to change color. Some of the maples were scarlet. How nice your little cottage looks."

At this point, she took some paper bags and baskets from the back seat of the car. The bags and baskets contained tomatoes, lettuce, green beans, summer squashes, and apples. Adam's mother grew the vegetables in her garden. The apples came from a small orchard that had been his father's pride. Adam carried the produce into the cottage and set it on the kitchen table. Then he brought out some chairs from the screen porch and placed them in the yard. The two women sat down. His mother was telling Margaret that the apple harvest promised to be the best ever this year, and that even the trees which had not been sprayed were laden with perfect fruit.

"I wish your father could have seen them," she said to Adam.

Adam looked at his mother. Though she was over sixty, there was still youth and sweetness in her face, and, as always, she wore her widowhood with serenity. Was it because of her religion? he wondered. When he had gone home, a year before, to attend his father's funeral, the house had been filled with friends from her church. He was relieved to find that she was not alone and that she had friends to comfort her, but, full of grief at his father's death, and on edge after the long, swift drive, he was unprepared to face the calmness of the faces that turned toward him when he entered the living room. "Your father was a fine Christian gentleman," one woman told him. "Was he?" Adam inquired politely. He knew that, except to admire certain French and German cathedrals, his father had not set foot in a church for more than fifty years. His father hated cant and loved life. He wept unashamedly at the deaths and funerals of friends. Adam had wept at his. Now, keeping an eye on little John, who was wandering happily about the yard, he heard his mother describing the variety of apples that grew in her orchard.

"The McIntoshes come early, of course, and then the Macouns. I've brought you some of both. My favorites are the Baldwins, though. They'll ripen toward the end of next month. Perhaps I could send you some."

The baby had moved toward the bushel basket containing the toadstools. Adam got to his feet, headed him off, and, taking his hand, coaxed him back to the vicinity of the chairs. His mother was telling Margaret about an insidious type of fruit fly that, in other years, had infested the apples with worms. Adam remembered his father walking through the orchard at evening, and, suddenly restless, took up the spade again and began to remove the remaining toadstools from the yard. Margaret went into the house to make some coffee, and for a time he could hear his mother playing with the baby. When he glanced at her a few minutes later, however, he found that she was looking at him intently.

"Adam," she inquired. "Whatever are you doing?"

When he told her, his mother smiled.

"D'you know what a toadstool is?" she asked.

"Sure," Adam replied. "It's a poisonous mushroom."

His mother shook her head. "Mycologists regard the toadstool and the mushroom as synonymous," she said. "In fact, there are edible toadstools and poisonous mushrooms, as well as vice versa."

"Well," Adam answered, "these smelly things certainly look poisonous, don't they? I wouldn't touch one on a bet."

"All fungi deteriorate rapidly," his mother went on. "They should be picked and eaten fresh. The same as vegetables. You know, of course, that one can be poisoned by rotten vegetables." Mrs. Foster paused, as if to affirm the incontestability of her point; then she got up from her chair, walked to the basket, and picked up one of the toadstools Adam had deposited there. After examining it closely, she held it to her nose and sniffed. *"Cantharellus cibarius,"* she announced. "It's more commonly known as the Chanterelle and it is entirely edible. I don't happen to prefer it because it tends to be tough and must be stewed for a long time. But many people seek it avidly."

Adam stuck his spade in the ground and looked at his mother with amazement. "How d'you know about mushrooms?" he asked.

"I've been studying them," she replied. "Mrs. Drummond at the garden club got me started. It's really quite fascinating and not anywhere as dangerous as many people seem to think. One just has to know the species and be able to differentiate them by their characteristics and the color of the spore dust that falls from their gills."

"Listen," Adam said, "I think it's an awfully dangerous hobby. The newspapers have been full of stories lately about people getting sick on wild mushrooms. Why, just last week a man and woman died of eating mushrooms on Long Island, and half a dozen other people wound up in hospitals."

"Obviously, they didn't know their mushrooms," Mrs. Foster replied with a smile. "They must have eaten one or another species of the genus *Amanita,* some of which, of course, are deadly."

"Who knows what they ate?" Adam retorted. "All I know is that the poison control center has issued a warning that the best way to prevent mushroom poisoning is not to gather or eat any of them."

"But of course they have, my dear. They have to do that in order to protect the great majority of people who simply won't take the trouble to study and learn. Suppose a certain kind of apple were found to be poisonous. Wouldn't the authorities warn everybody not to eat apples?"

Adam shook his head. "In my opinion, it's just not worth the risk," he said flatly.

"Adam, you shouldn't say things in such a positive manner. It sounds—well, it sounds ignorant."

Margaret had brought a tray containing coffee and cake out into the yard, and they all sat down again.

"I've just been telling Adam that these mushrooms he's been digging out of the yard are quite harmless," Mrs. Foster said brightly.

"Really!" Margaret exclaimed. "But they smell so terrible."

"That's because they've deteriorated, my dear."

"Which means I'm right not to want the baby to nibble at one of them," Adam said irritably.

"Yes, of course you are," his mother replied. "It's your general attitude about mushrooms I was commenting upon."

Margaret served the coffee and cake. "Whenever I hear of mushrooms, I always remember what happened to a friend of my family," she said. "He was an expert on mushrooms. He spoke about mushrooms at women's clubs and even wrote articles about them. Then, one day, he ate the wrong kind and died."

"You see," said Adam. "If the experts can make mistakes, it's simply not worth the risk."

"Adam," said his mother in the tone of voice she had always used when religion was discussed in their house, "you mustn't close your eyes to things."

After lunch, when the baby had been put away for his afternoon nap, Adam's mother announced that she was going to take a short walk in the woods. When she had gone, Adam cleared the dishes from the table, and Margaret began to wash them in the sink.

"Adam, try not to be hostile toward your mother," she said.

"Well, did you ever hear of such damned stubbornness? Why, she goes on about mushrooms as if she were reading from the Scriptures!"

"You can't change people," Margaret said. "Besides, you don't know very much about mushrooms *or* religion, do you?"

"What the hell!" Adam exclaimed. "Wasn't it your idea as well as mine to rid the yard of those rotten toadstools?"

"Yes," Margaret replied, "but why make an issue of it? There's a nice Mother Earth quality to your mother. She's got the greenest thumb I know, and she has a wonderful knowledge and love of nature. Don't ruin her visit over some silly mushrooms."

"Okay," Adam said. "Okay." He went out into the yard and, deliberately ignoring the spade, sat down and began to read the Sunday paper.

Half an hour later he heard his mother call his name.

She had come up quietly and was standing close behind him. "Adam," she said softly. "Adam, there's something I'd like very much to show you. Will you come?" There was a gentle, tentative persuasion in her voice, as if she expected him to refuse, or to make the kind of excuse he always made when she asked him to accompany her to church on Easter Sunday.

Adam heaved an inward sigh, got to his feet, and followed his mother out behind the cottage and into the woods. A year before, he had cleared several acres in this section of brush, thickets, and stunted saplings, and now the damp earth underfoot was carpeted with rotting leaves, patches of ground pine, and clumps of fern. As they passed the stump of a tree he had felled and cut up for firewood, his mother pointed to some fungi growing on its side. The fungi were a reddish chestnut color and were growing in overlapping tiers.

"*Polyporous lucidus*," his mother said. "Too tough and leathery for eating."

On they went, his mother leading, until they reached the far side of the clearing, where the forest began again in earnest. Here the ground sloped away toward a stream and grew even more moist because of water that seeped through the earth. Now, sure-footedly, Mrs. Foster descended the incline, made her way around a rotting, wind-fallen oak, and, pausing before a patch of bare, wet earth, pointed to a single snow-white mushroom that was growing out of it. The mushroom was eight inches tall and had the appearance of a miniature umbrella. The only imperfections in its shape were a small bulbous ring around the base of the stem and some slight scaling on

the top of the cap. Otherwise—solitary, still, and symmetrical—it stood dwarfed and delicate in the vast forest,
like the cottage itself.

"Isn't it lovely?" Mrs. Foster said.

"Yes," Adam replied. "It is."

"D'you have any idea what kind it is?"

Adam looked quickly at his mother. "No," he said.
"I don't."

For a moment his mother looked at him tenderly. "It
is an *Amanita virosa*," she said finally. "It is quite common, and it is deadly poison. It is so poisonous that its
toxin can only be disintegrated and destroyed by boiling
acids. Nor is time a factor. Specimens of *Amanita virosa*
have been known to retain their poison for periods up to
nine years. When eaten by humans, the poison attacks
and dissolves the blood corpuscles. The first symptoms
occur within ten hours and include severe abdominal
pains, vomiting, cramps in the limbs, convulsions, and a
weakening of the pulse. Death invariably follows within
two to four days. For this reason, and because it is so
beautiful, the *Amanita virosa* is called the Angel of
Death."

Adam glanced at the mushroom and then looked at his
mother again. To his horror, she was smiling slightly,
and there was a serenity in her face that could only, he
felt, reflect her profound acceptance and belief that everything in God's universe was as it should be, including
this deadly thing at his feet. For a second he wanted to
stamp the mushroom under his heel, but he knew that
there must be many in these woods, and that even if he
did, the evil spores would only sprout again. Suddenly,

he heard the screen door of the cottage slam and his child shouting with the joy of having awakened. Then, softer but still audible, he heard his wife's tender voice of admonishment. His mother was already climbing back up the incline toward the yard, and, helplessly, he followed in her wake.

The Snow in Petrograd   Matthew Springer
stood at a window in the Columbia Graduate Student
Lounge watching the snow fall and silently rehearsing the
remarks he would make when it came time for him to introduce Alexandrei Petramovitch, who was the evening's
speaker. *We of the Russian Institute are fortunate to have
with us tonight—* Springer cut himself off as, glancing in
the direction of the doorway, he saw that Petramovitch
had entered the room. The two men had never met, but
Springer had heard Petramovitch lecture at the Institute
in 1954, when the Cold War was still at its height.
Springer, who was now an instructor at the Institute, had
been a student at the time, Petramovitch was already an
old man, and the lecture had been memorable, for Petramovitch had electrified his audience by insisting, with
fiery eloquence, that, in spite of the excesses of Stalin,
Socialism was the only valid form of government for
Russia. Now, as Springer moved forward to greet him, he

185

found himself looking down at a pale little man whose threadbare overcoat and white goatee seemed not so much worn by his shrunken body and waxen face as hung from them. Only Petramovitch's eyes—blue, triangular, and set in his head like gable windows—appeared vital and life-size. His eyes are still full of revolutionary zeal, Springer thought. "It was good of you to come on such a stormy night," he said.

Petramovitch smiled, and the authentic eyes crinkled at the corners. "I am Russian," he replied in the heavily accented English that Springer remembered from a dozen years before. "I do not mind the snow."

Springer helped the old man out of his overcoat, led him to the speaker's lectern, and stood by his side as the last students and faculty members entered the room. The audience would not be as large as for the two previous lectures of the winter series—it had been standing room only for the man from the Soviet Embassy, and there had been a full house for an émigré count—but, considering the bad weather, Springer felt that the turnout was respectable. While he waited for the noise to subside, he told Petramovitch that he had read and enjoyed his most recent book. "I particularly liked the last section, where you speculate on the kind of Russian society that could have been constructed if the Mensheviks and other moderate Socialists had gained control of the Revolution," he said.

"I'm flattered," Petramovitch answered simply. "Also by this audience. That there should be so many people still interested in hearing about the Revolution pleases me."

186

"They're interested in hearing you," Springer said graciously. "After all, you were a participant."

"Ah, yes," said Petramovitch, smiling again. "An actor from an ancient history."

The room had settled down, and Springer took a final look at a white card upon which he had scribbled some biographical notes about his guest. "Alexandrei Petramovitch," he read. "Born in 1880, in Cracow. Educated at the University in Kiev. Delegate to the Stockholm Socialist Congress of 1906. Exiled from Russia in 1908 for activity against the czarist government. Returned after the March Revolution of 1917. Member of the Executive Committee of the Petrograd Soviet, and associate of Julius Martov, leader of the Menshevik wing of the Social Democratic Party. Left Russia for good after the Bolsheviks seized power. Lived in Paris until 1939. Author of several books on Russia, including *A Socialist's History of the Revolution,* and editor of *Sotsialisticheskii Vestnik,* official newspaper of the Social Democratic Labor Party in exile. *Tonight Mr. Petramovitch will give us his recollections of the Revolution of 1917 . . .*"

Applause for Petramovitch rose and fell as Springer finished his introduction and sat down at a table adjacent to the lectern. The old man acknowledged his audience with a nod and pulled on a pair of rimless glasses. "Could anyone have thought, in March of 1917, that the Russian people rising like a tidal wave would sweep away so quickly and so easily the Romanov Dynasty?" he began in a voice full of wonder. "Certainly not those of us in the various revolutionary movements. Not Lenin, who was living in Switzerland, or Trotsky, who was here in New York, or Martov and other Mensheviks like myself, who were scattered about Europe. No, we had not the slightest idea that the revolution was so near at hand. For years we exiles had been carrying on sterile quarrels amongst ourselves about how best to achieve a revolution in Russia, when suddenly it happened. I can tell you we were of two minds about it. We were happy, of course, yet we were also anxious, for now it was necessary to take action. But how to act? And what to do?"

Petramovitch paused and smiled apologetically at his listeners, as if he were inviting them to be amused at his ancient quandary; then he continued, wagging a forefinger beside his ear so that it seemed to be keeping time to some faint, familiar rhythm. "Martov went to Switzerland and proposed to Lenin that the revolutionary factions cease their quarreling and open negotiations with the Germans, in order that we might all be granted transportation back to Russia," he said. "It was Martov's idea, however, that we wait until permission was granted for our return by the provisional revolutionary government which had been proclaimed by the Duma Committee. In this way Martov hoped to affirm support for the March Revolution and for the creation of a stable democratic regime. . . ."

For Springer, these opening remarks contained a review of events and an outline of conditions with which he and the audience were wholly conversant. Was it because of this that he already sensed a hint of restlessness in the room—a slight squeaking among the folding chairs which foretold growing boredom? Springer recalled the

rapt attention that had been paid to the well-tailored
young man from the Soviet Embassy, who spoke with
bland assurance that the revised history that constituted
his text was unassailable, and to the tweedy White Russian count, whose hatred of Communism allowed him to
distort history to the extent of denying the basic validity
of the Revolution. It seemed a pity that the account of a
man who had not only been in Petrograd during the up-
heaval but even taken an important part in it should not
engender great interest. But the fire was gone from Petramovitch. His voice was lusterless. He was simply recount-
ing the history that could be found in textbooks. Springer
wondered if the old man had lived with his story so long
that he had become detached from it. He hoped that
Petramovitch would retrieve the situation by telling them
something personal about his experience in Petrograd.
What had he felt as he witnessed the cataclysm that shook
the world?

But for the next half hour Petramovitch was content
to carry his audience chronologically over the ups and
downs of the turbulent summer and autumn of 1917. He
told of the abortive *coup d'état* attempted by the
Kronstadt sailors; of the ebb in Bolshevik fortunes result-
ing from Lenin's subsequent flight to Finland and from
Trotsky's arrest; of the resurgence of the Bolsheviks in
September, after Kerensky released Trotsky and his fol-
lowers from prison to help stem a *coup d'état* by Kornilov
and the Rightists; of Lenin's dramatic return from Finland, when he smuggled himself incognito into Petrograd
by swathing his face in bandages; of the Bolshevik domi-
nation of the second All-Russian Congress of Soviets that

189

was convened in the Smolny Institute on the day after Trotsky's forces had seized the railroad stations, the telephone office, and the bridges across the Neva; and, finally, of Julius Martov rising bravely to his feet and being howled down by the Bolsheviks as he denounced them for plunging the country into civil war.

At this point, lulled by Petramovitch's narrative as he might have been by one of those symphonies that are too well known to hold surprises, Springer was startled to hear the old man's voice rise in fervent crescendo as he launched into a tribute to Martov. "Do not forget Julius Martov!" Petramovitch cried. "Martov was a Socialist who stood not only for the Revolution but for democracy as well. He would never have acceded to the repressions that were undertaken to implement the early five-year plans. He would have—" Petramovitch broke off and, as if groping for a phrase, turned away from his audience and looked out the window. He remained silent for so long a time that Springer began to wonder if—sidetracked by senility and lost in contemplation of the falling snow—he had forgotten his train of thought. But then, to his relief, the old man turned back and smiled his apologetic smile. "It is too late, I think, to talk about what Martov would have done," he said with a shrug. "Martov has been gone a long time. He died in exile in Berlin, more than forty years ago. If time and biology permit, however, I hope one day to write a biography of him. As for what happened in Petrograd, we were amateurs. Yes, that's what it amounted to in the end. We Mensheviks were amateurs and our adversaries were professionals."

For some moments the audience was uncertain

whether Petramovitch had concluded his remarks with
this admission or merely lapsed into another silence. A
first tentative handclap came when the old man began to
gather up his notes from the lectern, but the audience had
been caught off balance, and the applause that followed
was sporadic and of short duration. After it had died
away, Springer got up and moved to the lectern to an-
nounce that there was time for a few questions from the
floor. When he glanced at Petramovitch, however, he saw
that the old man's face was sagging with fatigue. "It's not
necessary to have the question-and-answer period,"
Springer whispered. "Perhaps you would like to call it a
night."

"If you don't mind," Petramovitch replied. "I have
grown very tired."

When Petramovitch and Springer left the student
center, some minutes later, it was still snowing. The snow
was six inches deep on the sidewalk, and the footing beneath was slippery. Springer took the old man by the arm,
and the two of them proceeded very slowly, across a
deserted quadrangle, toward Amsterdam Avenue, where
Springer planned to hail a cab. As they walked, Springer
thanked his guest for coming and complimented him on
his talk, but Petramovitch made no reply, and for several
minutes they struggled on through the snow in awkward
silence. Springer wondered if Petramovitch was down-
cast because of his lapse at the lectern, or if he regretted
the harsh admission with which he had terminated his
lecture, and, tangled in these considerations, he was suddenly overcome with compassion for this aging man who,

pressed by time and biology, had ventured out on a stormy night to impart recollections that were nearly half a century old. He wanted to say something encouraging to Petramovitch—something to the effect that, successful or not, he was more fortunate than most men to have stood at a watershed of history and to have had a chance to divert the flow of events. But Springer did not; it seemed too patronizing. Instead, to fill the silence, he asked Petramovitch what it was he had forgotten toward the end of his lecture. "It was when you turned and looked out the window," Springer went on with a smile. "I thought you were trying to remember something about Martov."

. Petramovitch stopped in his tracks and gave the younger man a look of profound reproach. "My friend, when you are as old as I am, you will not always be forgetting things," he replied. "Sometimes you will remember things you had forgotten long before. This evening, after so many years in other countries, I looked out the window at the snow falling past dark buildings and suddenly found I was remembering the night I left the Smolny for the last time. It was a week or so after Martov's courageous speech, and the first snow of the year was falling in Petrograd. The city was transformed. For the first time in months, everything was still." Petramovitch took Springer's arm, and they continued across the silent quadrangle. "The stillness was frightening, for I was heartsick at our failure and afraid for what was going to happen in Russia," the old man went on. "But as I walked through the deserted streets of Petrograd, I was filled with a strange kind of peace. Of course, it was not peace I felt, but resignation. Yes, I was like a frightened man alone in bed in a dark house, and it was as if the snow were a blanket that I had pulled over my head before going to sleep."

Hydrography

On the fourth day—Thursday—they retraced their steps. It was, he had convinced her, the best solution. He did not really have to convince her, for they had agreed quietly and quickly about everything they had undertaken in those four days. Yet he was aware that it was he who had proposed what they would do now and she who had agreed to it. Would his grief betray them in the future? he wondered. No matter, since they had no choice to begin with. To retrieve what was left and to relinquish it—that was not choice but necessity.

The mausoleum, a block of granite surrounded by a large cemetery, was half an hour's drive from the city. The cemetery was filled with evergreens that, even in midwinter, lent it the aura of a formal garden. He parked the car in front of the mausoleum and, leaving her inside, climbed out, mounted a flight of stone steps, and went into the building through a pair of massive-looking portals which, because they were fake bronze, opened with deceptive ease. Inside, his footsteps echoed on a polished marble floor with the same hammering precision he had heard two days before, when he had been led down a succession of long, drafty corridors to the crematory at the rear of the building. This time his stay was brief. He presented himself at an office, where the sound of his approach died with stunning abruptness on wall-to-wall carpeting. He identified himself to a clerk wearing a black suit, signed a receipt, and was handed a small, square box wrapped in brown paper. The box was feather light. A white label on the cover bore the name of his son. When he left the office, the sound of his footsteps followed him again to the fake bronze doors. It was raining outside, as it had been all day, but now the rain was mixed with sleet and snow.

The cemetery was deserted and—because of this, perhaps—the Muzak loudspeaker affixed to the wall of the building behind a screen of evergreens was mercifully silent. He descended the stone steps, holding the box carefully between his hands, and saw for the first time that the cemetery was sprinkled with bouquets withering beneath the leaden February sky. Then, as if seeking confirmation for what was being done, his eyes sought her face behind the rain-streaked window of the car. Could he bear to watch her in the coming years—she who loved plants and flowers—tending them beside a tiny grave? No, nor would he and she come bearing floral tributes to one of the tenement cemeteries that sat beside expressways on the outskirts of the city, or to such a place as this, where, on sunny days, recorded hymns came piping through the crackle of static. They had made the right decision, and they had agreed upon it. Now it simply remained to carry it out. All at once he was filled with vast relief that, for the first time in four days, they were—all three of them— alone again, unseparated by the legal barriers of state and county and by the presence of clergy, family, and friends. When he reached the car, he opened the door and placed the box on the rear seat beside a rose she had taken from one of the funeral bouquets. Then he got in behind the wheel. Except for memory, there must be no shrine, he told himself. No shrine.

For the next hour they drove swiftly north and east, re-tracing their route of four days before. During the first part of the trip the highway followed a small river that wandered between giant willow trees. Then they passed a series of reservoirs in the northern part of the county, linked together by streams whose flow was controlled by dams. The river and the streams flowed toward them, in the direction of the city and the sea, and as they sped along—always against the current and backward in time —the idea kept recurring to him that they were climbing toward headwaters, where the purest spring-fed trickles crept out of the hills. Now, as the roads diminished in proportion to the narrowing of the streams, he became more aware than ever of going back, of returning to the very source of things. The reverie was broken when, ap-proaching the state line, he slowed at a fork in the road, thinking to take an alternate route that would spare them the sight of the town through whose dark, uncharted streets they had careered wildly, four nights before, in a vain effort to find a doctor to save their dying child. But even as he pressed his foot against the brake, she spoke for almost the first time since they had left the city. "Don't turn," she said. "Let's go the way we always did."

Twenty minutes later they reached the cottage where they had always spent their weekends. The cottage sat like a balcony in the forest, on a high, wooded ridge adjacent to the Housatonic Valley, where—tiny, white, and clapboarded—it was dwarfed by tall trees and surrounded by stone walls. Thus enclosed, it tended to seem gloomy and additionally submerged on such gray winter days as this, when sodden snowflakes came slanting past the trunks of trees. Only her ivy plants, carefully transplanted and nurtured over the years, and clinging forlorn and faintly green to the side of the cottage, held a trace of life. The rest was gray—gray stone, gray sod, gray tree trunks—all becoming grayer now as the snow began to stick.

They did not enter the house, but pulled on their galoshes in the car. In the spring he would come back alone to put away the toys. Now he took the box from the back seat, unwrapped the paper covering, and drew out a small canister; then, handing her the rose, he got out, came around to her side, and opened the door. The hand she gave him was as light as the canister, and, taking it, he led her across the spongy yard and along a path through the forest to the brook.

The brook was a torrent. Fed by old snow melting at the top of the hill, it tumbled between boulders covered with gray lichen and raced down shale-lined runways, coating thickets with shining ice and carving a gully that would, with time, become a ravine. He had already picked the spot in his mind. Now, kneeling on a flat rock where the brook spilled into a deep pool, he opened the canister and poured its meager contents into the swift current. For a moment there was a small white stain in the dark water of the pool—a stain that, even as it spread, dissolved and disappeared. The rose she tossed upon the water was borne lightly along, cresting with absurd buoyance as it tumbled over the rocks. Lost from sight, it reappeared; an instant later it was gone.

He looked up at her, saw the deprivation in her face, and was filled with doubt. But even as he stood and took her hand again, his spirit fled from the spot and followed the brook as it flowed away. Below the hill, in the meadow where he sometimes fished for trout, he traced it past its conjunction with other rivulets and other brooks. He followed it through the culvert beneath the highway, past the millhouse near the railroad tracks, and then down, down, always down, through fields and forests to the river. At first the river was a series of lakes created by flood-control dams; then it spilled through the giant portals of a hydroelectric plant and flowed past summer cottages and factories into the flatlands near the coast, where white motorboats bobbed at marinas. There the river emptied into the sound, and the sound into the sea, and, drawing a deep breath, he returned in one jump to the headwaters where they stood. The continuity of his journey had calmed him. Did she not seem calmer, too? Helping her up the bank, he led her back to the car, which wore a coat of snow.

The drive back to the city seemed swifter, as if they were being helped along by favorable currents. The narrow country roads widened into arteries bearing median markings, and then into multi-laned highways, until they found themselves carried along in a stream of traffic that flowed beside the Hudson. That night, lying awake, he began to follow the brook once more from the top of the hill. Again and again he traced its descent through the countryside. Once he had seen a topographic map of Connecticut, and now his mind carried him through countless flesh folds of the land. Trickles became brooks, brooks became streams, streams widened into rivers. The rivers flowed into the sea. His brain was awash with currents that coursed through the wrinkled contours of vast watersheds. Whole continents drained through his head. Everything emptied into the sea. The sea was empty. He began again.

Two nights later they crossed the ocean on the nine-o'clock Alitalia flight to Rome. When she seemed to have fallen asleep, he sat staring out a window into the dark, and thought of the profound sea pulsing forty thousand feet below them. Day broke as they approached the coast of France, but the land was covered with a thick layer of clouds. In his mind, however, he pursued the course of the Loire, along which he had driven years before. Later he imagined they were flying above the confluence of the Saône and Rhone. The cloud cover diminished over Switzerland. In valleys between the Alps the rivers and streams were frozen and white. He followed them eagerly, craning his neck and looking back beyond the wing, hating to lose them even as they disappeared behind the towering ranges. Italy was green and brown. In the

Lombard plain the ancient tributaries of the Po flowed through the coils of their discarded meanders. The Mediterranean gently lapped the Tuscan coast. When they landed in Rome, they went to a hotel and slept.

When they awoke, they walked. They walked along the Tiber, which was a green-gray color and very high. (He supposed, with an attendant journey in his mind, that it was being flooded by snow melting high up in the Apennines.) They continued walking all week, pausing occasionally to consult a Hachette Guide, and everywhere they went she cut sprigs of ivy. She cut them from ruined stones in the Forum, from chariot ruts in the Colosseum, from beds in the Borghese Gardens, and from the walls of the Vatican Museum. In the evenings, when they returned to the hotel, she put the sprigs in a glass of water on their bureau. At the end of the week, when they left by bus for Florence, she wrapped the sprigs in moist paper, placed them in a plastic sack, and stuck them in her handbag.

The bus went to Florence by way of Assisi, where she added to her collection of ivy by snipping a shoot from the walls of a monastery. In Florence they did an extraordinary amount of walking. They walked along the Arno, which he was surprised to find muddy and full of shoals, and down innumerable corridors of the Pitti Palace and the Uffizi Gallery. She found lovely ivy in the Boboli Gardens, and on the last day, after they had climbed up the stone steps to the Piazzale Michelangelo, from which they could see the summits of the Apennines on one side and the plain of Florence on the other, he saw her as he stood by the railing—his mind unreeling from his body like a fishing line from its spool—smile for the first time in days as she stooped to cut another sprig from a vine that grew along the staircase.

When they returned to Rome, by train, the sack of ivy bulged her handbag. During the trip the leaves of some of the older shoots began to droop, but she managed to sustain them by keeping the paper moist. That evening they flew to Catania, where his brother met them at the airport. His brother was a land-use expert who had been in Sicily a year, donating *pasta* and dispensing farm equipment in behalf of a government-aid program. Tall, frail, and somber in expression, he grasped each of them by the arm and steered them through a noisy crowd in the terminal building; then he drove them to a hotel that was situated on the lower slopes of Mount Etna. Before they went to bed, she carefully arranged her ivy in a water pitcher. The sprigs were holding their own. Tiny white shoots had already begun to sprout from some of the stems. She pointed them out to him joyfully.

During the following week his brother took them sightseeing. His brother was well versed in the history of Sicily, and, glad to be free of the Biblically fine print of the Hachette Guide, they surrendered themselves gratefully to his knowledge. At Syracuse they ate a picnic lunch in the ruins of the Fort of Euryelus, and she plucked ivy from the quarry walls of the Latomia del Paradiso. At Gela they examined some Greek walls dating from the fifth century, but she found no ivy growing there. At Agrigento they spent a morning wandering through the Valley of the Temples in a driving rain. At noon they returned to their hotel, thoroughly drenched, and found the water pitcher on the bureau empty and all her ivy gone.

She burst into tears and flung herself upon the bed. He rushed out into the corridor, seized a startled chambermaid by the arm, and brought her back. His puzzled brother translated. The ivy was fading, the maid explained. Naturally, she assumed the Signora had no use for it, but perhaps the porter would remember if he had thrown it out. He went off to find the porter. The porter shrugged at his story, but when he drew a thousand-lira note from his wallet, the man took him into a yard behind the hotel, rummaged through a trash basket, and pulled out the ivy, which was in a paper bag. He bore it back to her in triumph.

Before leaving Agrigento, he bought a large glass jar, and, safely ensconced in water, the ivy was placed on the floor beneath the back seat of his brother's car. They drove to Caltanissetta and then to Enna, through a barren land filled with grim rock, dead turf, and dry gulches. The rain gave way to cold mist as they climbed higher, and they drove through incredibly poor mountain villages where miserable stone houses soaked up the damp like blocks of pumice and a chill wind whipped the spindly legs of undernourished, ill-clad children. He only half listened as his brother enumerated the reasons for the awful poverty; he was hoping that the sight of the children would not sadden her further, but even as he did, he found himself wandering endlessly, helplessly through steep gorges. He imagined raindrops forming tiny puddles that, overflowing, became trickles that, swelling, grew into rivulets, brooks, and torrents, which, merging now, plunged down into green valleys past hillsides dotted with grazing sheep and the ruins of ancient temples toward the sea. . . .

Bitterly, his brother explained the frustrations that attended his work. One of the chief problems was the sad neglect of the land. *"Pasta,* tractors—it's just stopgap stuff," his brother said. "What's needed is a real program of reforestation and agrarian education. The trouble is the peasants are filled with hopelessness. Ignorance, the Mafia, government corruption, overpopulation—" Having uttered the word, his brother cast a quick glance at him and broke off with a shrug.

They spent the night and part of the next day in Enna. It was still raining when they left, late in the afternoon, but the rain had diminished somewhat by the time they reached the western slopes of Mount Etna, and his brother suggested they circle north around the mountain, stay the night at Randazzo, and delay their return to Catania for another day; he promised to show them some remarkable scenery. They agreed, and drove on over a narrow, tortuous road that wound around great flows of lava and passed through dark towns that seemed darker for having been constructed of the same scorched rock.

In the morning the sun was shining. As they continued their detour around the mountain, they could see snow fields high up on the truncated cone of the volcano, and a dark-green belt of pines beneath, where the tree line ended. When they reached the Mediterranean side, the sun was high in the sky, and the land sloping away to the shining blue-green sea was splashed with groves of lemon trees. His brother parked the car at a vantage point, and

they climbed out to take in the view at leisure. To the
north, toward Taormina, the coast stretched away in
spectacularly jagged fashion. Then his brother pointed to
a place directly below them, between the towns of Fiume-
freddo and Riposto, where there was an immense brown
stain upon the sea. The stain seemed to be propelled by
some great force, and, even as he looked along his brother's outstretched arm, he saw it spreading, merging with
the green water, and changing shape in the wind and current.

His brother told him that it marked the mouth of a
stream that began not far from where they were standing.
Then he pointed out the course of the stream, which ran
through hidden defiles in the lava deposits, through
lemon groves and villages, and across a stretch of sandy
bottomland before it reached the sea. "There's a perfect
example of what I was telling you yesterday," his brother
said quietly. "Some years ago, the government planted
trees along the entire course of the stream to hold the
earth in place. But as fast as the seedlings were put into
the ground, they were eaten up by goats and sheep. It's
the story of Sicily. No one ever cares in time, and the best
soil has long ago washed out to sea."

For a long while he stood rooted to the spot, and
watched the stain spreading over the azure water. Only
with an immense effort did he resist the temptation to
escape, to begin tracing the slow, quickening, and then
endlessly racing descent of still another stream. Finally,
when he turned around, stricken with doubt and fully expecting to find in her face that look of deprivation which,
defying the erosion of all geological time, could only be

matched by the despair in his heart, she was not there. She had crossed to the other side of the roadway, where, kneeling beside a low retaining wall—a tiny stone wall that seemed incredibly frail against the vast thrust of the mountain—she was cutting yet another sprig of ivy.

Paul Brodeur

Paul Brodeur was born in 1931, in Boston. He was
graduated from Harvard College, served in the Counter
Intelligence Corps in Germany, and since 1958 has been
a writer on the staff of *The New Yorker,* to which he has
contributed short stories and many nonfiction pieces. His
first novel, *The Sick Fox,* was published to critical
acclaim in 1963, and *The Stunt Man,* his second novel,
published by Atheneum in 1970, is available in British,
French, Italian, and Japanese editions.